'Whatever is she thinking about?'

'She's thinking we both have good singing voices for a duet,' he said, smiling broadly. 'It'll be perfectly all right, you know.' He gave his lantern a hitch. 'We're unlikely to be slow-handclapped, not on Christmas Eve.' And he fell into line at the back of the choir.

'He fancies you rotten,' Chrissie said *sotto voce* to Jill. 'Half the nursing staff would like to be in your shoes tonight.'

'I'm singing with him, not sleeping with him!' Jill was quick to retort, but Chrissie only giggled.

Janet Ferguson was born at Newmarket, Suffolk. She nursed as a VAD during the Second World War, then became a medical secretary working in hospitals in London and the provinces, and in Sussex, where she now lives. She has had a number of novels published—several of them being Medical Romances

Previous Titles

OPTICAL ILLUSION
CALLING DOCTOR IVER

ENCOUNTER WITH A SURGEON

BY

JANET FERGUSON

MILLS & BOON LIMITED
ETON HOUSE   18–24 PARADISE ROAD
RICHMOND   SURREY   TW9 1SR

First published in Great Britain 1992 by Mills & Boon Limited

© Janet Ferguson 1992

Australian copyright 1992 Philippine copyright 1992 This edition 1992

ISBN 0 263 77632 8

Set in 10 on 11 pt Linotron Plantin 03-9204-60528 Typeset in Great Britain by Centracet, Cambridge Made and printed in Great Britain

CHAPTER ONE

'It's a mountain bike, one of those pricey jobs.' Dick moved the bright-coloured machine away from the wall and inspected it carefully, so far as he could, in the dimmish lights of the hospital yard.

'Oh, come on, Dick, put it back,' Jill urged. It was a bitter night in mid-December, and all she wanted was to reach Cade House—the nurses' home—and walk into blissful warmth.

The thing was, she hadn't been all that keen to go out in the first place, but Chrissie Anderson, her flatmate, was away, so, telling herself that nurses were supposed to have fun in their off-duty times, she had given way to persuasion and gone with Dick to a wine bar just off the Farringdon Road. Now he had found this stupid bike propped against the wall just beyond the entrance to Casualty, and, by the looks of him, was so intrigued that he couldn't leave it alone. Men are little boys ever, she thought, her eyes on his crouching form.

At twenty-five, however, Dick was a year older than her. He was the houseman on the surgical floor where Jill was a senior staff nurse. Their talk this evening had been mainly about the new registrar, Adam Greerson, who was due to take up his post in the morning. Jill hadn't yet met him, but Dick had, and thought he seemed all right. 'Anyway, I have to get on with him, don't I?' he'd said, and Jill had agreed.

'Come on, Dick, shift,' she urged him, and wasn't at all pleased when, taking no notice, he got on the bike and rode it, carefully at first, then hell for leather, along the narrow path between the boundary wall and the start of the car park—at present packed with cars. He went up as far as the end of the park, did a nifty U-turn and came pedalling back, his breath puffing steam into the frosty air.

'It's brilliant!' He braked and got off, grinning all over his face. 'Your turn, you have a go,' and he handed her the bike.

'You have to be joking!' She held it awkwardly, hating the feel of it.

'Oh, come on, Jill, don't be chicken—give yourself a thrill. It's a terrific job, utterly different from an ordinary machine.'

'That I can well believe!' She started to wheel it back to the wall. 'I've not ridden a bike since I was at school, and this one isn't ours. You seem to have forgotten that important little fact.'

'All, the same, try it.'

'No.'

'I dare you.'

'Don't be silly, Dick.'

'All right, then, how about this?' He gave the bike a pat. 'If you can ride it up to where I did and back, without falling off, I'll buy the whole of that book of draw tickets you're selling for the orphans' fund.'

She turned round slowly, trying to see his face, trying to see if he really meant it. 'Is that a promise?' she asked.

'Absolutely. . .firm as a rock. . .*and* it's a good offer.'

She nodded, for she knew it was; it was a very good offer indeed. It would cost him ten pounds, and for the orphans' fund she was willing to take a risk.

'Well, come on, are you game?' he asked her. She hesitated no more.

'All right, then, for the good of the cause. . .anything!' she laughed, and Dick held the machine while she got on, for she might as well get a good start.

But the second she was on it and pedalling like mad

she knew she had made a mistake. Her jeans were too tight, and the saddle too hard, and the handlebars wouldn't keep straight. She'd been crazy to try it—she'd fall off any minute; she was wobbling all over the place. Once she swerved too far to the right and narrowly missed the line of parked cars crouching there in the dark. Supposing she'd hit one, supposing she had. . . It was the doctors' car park too. She started to sweat, in spite of the cold, and when she made the turn at the top to get on to the home stretch, and pedal back to Dick, the bike keeled over at shocking angle, exactly like a yacht.

She was still in the saddle, though; she hadn't fallen off. She was thinking this with a little bounce of pure satisfaction when she saw a man a few yards ahead of her, bending to one of the cars. Dear heaven, where had he come from, and so suddenly, right in her path? There were no lights on the bike—he hadn't seen her—and the brakes were too stiff to work. Jill panicked, stopped pedalling, but still plunged on—she couldn't, couldn't stop. She shrieked a warning, but left it too late. He turned and she hit him. . .and then she was off, lying on the path, the bike on top of her.

There was no sound from either of them at first; there was silence, broken only by the faint buzz of the bike's helplessly spinning wheels. Jill was jolted, though unhurt, but what of him, what of the man she'd run into? As she struggled to get up she saw him above her, lifting the bike off her legs, flinging it on to one side, bending to pull her up. 'Are you hurt?' he jerked, close to her face.

'No, but are you. . .are you all right?' she asked, and he let her go at once. 'I'm so sorry,' she babbled, 'I really *am* sorry—I do hope you're not hurt.' His face stopped her, the expression on it—she could see it by the lights of his car. He was suffused with rage, contorted with it, he appeared to have lost his breath. Jill lost hers too. Who was he, and what was he going to say. . .and where was Dick? Oh, where was Dick? Surely he'd come to her aid?

'May I ask what you're doing on hospital premises. . .riding a bike—at this time of night?' His voice started low, but rose up as it went on. 'You could have broken my leg, and your own neck—you could have seriously injured a member of staff. Who the devil are you?' He swung her round to the light.

'I *am* a member of staff. I have every right to be on the premises!' She was in the wrong, but his tone of voice stung, and one of her elbows felt bruised.

'Not on that machine you're not!' He watched her pick it up.

'It's not my bike; I was just trying it.' She very nearly said she was fund-raising, but stopped in time, for he might think she was mad. Dick had taken himself off, she knew that now; he wasn't going to help her. 'I was just trying it,' she said again.

'Joy-riding, in other words!'

'I wasn't enjoying it.'

He snorted—she heard him. He turned his back to unlock his car. He winced as he slid behind the wheel, and she heard that too. 'Put that bike back where you found it,' he said, 'then cut off home.' He held the door partly open, looking out at her—at her boyish figure in skin-tight jeans, bulging anorak and woolly ski-cap— setting the bike by the wall. 'Have you far to go?' He snapped out the question.

'I live in. . .at the nurses' home.' And now she heard him click the door shut. He was about to drive off the park. Well, thank goodness for that, thank goodness for no more questions or ticking-off. She was at the end of her endurance; she felt that if he'd gone on she'd have broken down and howled in front of him, or been impossibly rude.

He switched on the engine and it started to purr; it was a very opulent car. Jill could see him plainly in its lighted interior—a broad-shouldered man, with a long, lean, angular face, under thick reddish-brown hair. She didn't think he was one of the Walbrook's doctors, for she'd never seen him before, and as it was late, and he was about to drive *off* the precinct instead of on, he was most likely a visiting doctor, or a friend of one of the residents. . .not one of our crowd, she thought with a sigh of relief.

But he was rolling the window down enough to speak through, to deliver his parting shot. 'It strikes me you have a lot to learn if you're going to be a nurse. Academic achievement isn't enough; common sense and a sense of responsibility claim parity with that. You may be only just out of the schoolroom, but you should have learned that by now!' As he let in the clutch, his damaged ankle gave a red-hot leap, spurring him on to tell her to try to act like an adult.

He closed the window, leaving her speechless on the other side of it. She looked more like fifteen than eighteen in that ridiculous woollen cap. How in Hades had she ever got a place in a London nursing school? He faced front, not looking at her, then, reversing and turning, he drove off the park, out of the gates and down Smithfield Street, down towards Ludgate Hill, and the West End.

No sooner had he gone than Dick reappeared, and Jill could have throttled him. 'You rat, Dick! You absolute rat!' She leaned against the wall, rubbing her bashed elbow, shivering with nerves and cold.

'Don't be like that.' He looked closely at her. 'I couldn't show myself. I mean, what was the point? We'd both have been for it!'

'Very gallant, I'm sure!' She began to walk on, and he

kept pace with her. He lived at the doctors' residence, which was near to the nurses' home.

'Let me explain, Jill. I've got to tell you who that was, then you'll see. . .understand.' He took her arm, but she shook it free again. They were passing the brightly lit front of Casualty, entering the easterly yard, were within yards of their destination when she turned to him at last.

'Well, all right, then, who was it? Surprise me!' she asked.

'It was Greerson—Adam Greerson.'

'*What*?' She stumbled and nearly fell.

'Now do you see why I couldn't come and take part of the blame?'

'Adam Greerson!' She was still in shock, and could see nothing now but a vision of a tall man with thick fair brows and angry eyes, and a leg that hurt him. 'Oh, Dick, how terrible!'

'Yes, and he's my immediate boss, or will be as from tomorrow. He'd have got a shocking impression of me if I'd told him what we were up to—*owned* up, I mean, just to get you off the hook. I have to think of getting on, Jill; I have to stand well in his eyes. One day I hope to be a registrar myself. Tell me you understand.'

'What I understand,' she said through quivering lips, 'is that I have to see him. . .meet him on the ward. He thought I was a learner, and a very unsuitable one. He made that plain—he was very rude, and I was rude to him!'

Desperately she tried to recall what she'd said. Perhaps, after all, she hadn't been *too* rude, not in actual words. The worst thing was that she'd injured him— hurt his leg, or foot, or both. And he was a surgeon, needing to stand for absolute hours in Theatre.

'It's all your fault, Dick!' This was childish and she knew it.

'Oh, come off it, Jill! You didn't have to get on that

bike, you know. I didn't twist your arm, or get out my thumbscrews, which I never go out without!'

She said nothing to this, but as they walked on she began to see Dick's point of view. It *would* have looked bad if he'd popped up and confessed to his part in the crime. It would have been bad for him and, in the end, not a lot better for her. All it would have done was convince Mr Steely Adam Greerson that there were two nut-cases on the surgical floor instead of only one.

If he has, she thought sadly, to think ill of one of us perhaps it's better that it's me, for I don't come under his jurisdiction in the way that Dick does. I shall have to meet him, though, and look after his patients, and fill in when Sister's off duty. What is he going to say when he sees who the senior staff nurse is? She quailed at the thought, then another rose hopefully to the surface—with a bit of luck, a mere soupçon of luck, he might not recognise her. She looked very different in uniform, and it had been darkish in the yard. True, he had stared intently at her, but she was no traffic-stopper, so why should he remember her after tonight?

'I'm beginning to feel more cheerful,' she said, threading her arm through Dick's. She was rewarded by his telling her that she'd more than earned the ten pounds for the orphans' fund, and when they said goodnight on the steps of Cade House he thrust the note into her hand.

The flat in Cade House that Jill shared with Christabel Anderson comprised two bed-sitting-rooms, a shared kitchen and bathroom, up on the second floor. She could have done with her friend's company tonight, for Chrissie would very soon have put her straight and bucked her up, yet commiserated as well.

Still, at least I've got the bathroom to myself, she thought as she ran a deep bath and soaked in it, trying to avoid any stiffening-up after her fall. She had come off lightly, she decided, apart from her grazed elbow.

But what of him, she wondered, what of Adam Greerson? Perhaps he ought to have gone along to Casualty, just to be checked up. 'Damn him, he's old enough to know that for himself,' she said out loud, viciously soaping a foot. Even allowing for the shock of being run into, he'd been impossibly rude. He was the arrogant type, the chauvinistic type, who treated women like fools. She decided he was married and lived out somewhere—at Highbury, perhaps. He'd hardly have been driving *off* the precinct at eleven o'clock at night if he lived in at the doctors' residence. She ought to have asked Dick. Not that it mattered, of course. What mattered. . .and once again, she quailed at the thought. . .was meeting him on duty tomorrow, looking him in the eye, and praying that no light of recognition would flicker into it. No, I'm not that girl who was haring about on a bike in the yard last night; I don't look a bit like her, do I? You can see that for yourself.

Half an hour later, wakeful in bed, she lay in the darkness, listening to the sounds of London at night— to the chiming of City clocks, to the throb of late traffic, to the hoot of a tug on the river; to nearer-in sounds down in the yard—the opening and closing of doors, subdued voices, soft footfalls and, occasionally, a shout. There were times when Jill could hardly believe she had actually made it to London, that she was here at one of the major hospitals and nursing on Ecclestone Ward.

She had been at the Walbrook just on a year, having come from the Bexford General in Hertfordshire, where she'd done her training and staffed for two years on the wards. And life hadn't been easy for her during that time, for her parents had been killed in a train accident when she'd been in her second year of training. It had been a struggle to carry on after that, a struggle to pass her exams, but pass them she had, with flying colours, greatly helped by the supportive presence of her grandmother, Anna Stevens, who had sold her house in Cornwall and had come to live in Hertfordshire in the family home, which had been bequeathed to Jill.

So in time everything had rocked back on to an even keel. She had got this job at the Walbrook, had made friends of both sexes—good friends too—and she loved her work, into which she put her heart and soul, for Jill was the caring kind.

But now—she punched her pillow, trying to get to sleep—now she felt. . .well, not threatened exactly, but disturbed and unsettled. Things were going to change, she felt sure of that, and the change would be drastic. . .and alarming. . .and she wasn't prepared for that.

She was on the lates shift next morning, which meant that she would work from midday until nine o'clock at night. She didn't, therefore, have to get up early, which was a blessing because sleep eluded her until nearly four a.m. By twelve noon, however, she was crossing the yard, not quite so full of foreboding as last night, but not carefree either. Would he know her. . .would he recognise her? The wind was a spiteful one, and, ducking her head to keep her cap on, huddling her arms in her cape, she told herself to take courage. Adam Greerson was only a man.

The wind tugged at her cape, flapping it back to show the scarlet lining—red for Christmas, red like the holly berries; why, even the wind was telling her to be upstanding and rejoice in the time of year. Jill smiled to herself, remembering that this was the day when the trees would arrive. They had probably got here by now, load after load of them—dark green pine-scented firs, redolent of yule-tide, and the New Year, the season of goodwill. Nothing can alter Christmas, she thought, and I love it, I really do. Quickening her pace, she approached the glass doors of A and E, which glided apart to admit her, then closed with a noiseless gulp.

Ecclestone Ward, which was three floors up, was women's surgical. It was the old type of Nightingale ward, twenty-eight-bedded, and always full to overflowing, which meant that the four side-wards were very often brought into use as well. The throughput was swift, though, bewilderingly so at times, for, provided patients recovered well from surgery, and were free of drips and drains, they were discharged home after four or five days with their stitches still *in situ*, these being removed later by the visiting community nurse. This had the effect of scything more swiftly through the waiting list, but tended to prevent the nursing staff getting to know their patients, or even to establish much rapport.

A pale spear of winter sunshine gleamed across the wash-basins as, after taking off her cloak, Jill bent to wash her hands. Her reflection looked back at her from the mirror—a reflection that showed a slender girl in a white cotton dress belted with navy blue. Her gold hair was styled in a curving bob, her mouth was full and sweet, her nose tip-tilted, her eyes a warm hazel-brown. She was straightening her cap and changing into her ward shoes, when one of the third-year nurses—Rachel Marks—opened the door and came in.

'The new reg is here, Staff.' She joined Jill at the mirrors. 'He's in the ward now with Sir Rodney and Dick. He's absolutely *gorgeous*! You go in and see him— you'll never believe your eyes!'

'I expect I will.' A *frisson* of chill washed over Jill's shoulder-blades as she straightened up and went to the door. 'But fancy him coming in the middle of lunches— I can imagine what Sister said.'

'I think she's bowled over.' Rachel grinned as she banged her way into the loo.

Jill left the cloakroom and walked down the corridor to Sister's office. There was always paperwork to be done, and she sat down at the desk, facing the window, called a viewing window, which overlooked the ward. Lunches were being served out from a big heated trolley by Nurse Bell, assisted by June Sibley, the young learner nurse. Most patients had wooden trays slung across their beds, some were being helped to drink from spouted feeding-cups, others were eating at a communal table up at the day-room end. A tall Christmas tree, obviously one of the load delivered that morning, stood, starkly green and, as yet, untrimmed, to the right of the day-room doors. It was in front of this that Sister Beck and the new surgeon were standing. Sir Rodney Elverton, the consultant, and Dick were a pace or two away. All this Jill saw, but it was to Adam Greerson that her nervous gaze returned. She felt—and she could see him more plainly than last night—that he suited his name, his profile and posture were decidedly Adam-like. His hair was copper-beech-brown, she decided, he was around six feet tall, ruler-straight in his long white coat, shoulders square and broad. As she watched him she saw him fold his arms and lean back a little. He was talking to Sister, who was nodding so hard at something he was saying that Jill feared for her cap—the high, tucked muslin sort.

But they were turning round; they were coming out; they were facing the doors. Sir Rodney and Dick walked with them; they were passing the viewing window. Jill could hear the murmur of their voices as she bent her head, sorting reports. They wouldn't come into the office, she was sure; they would be off to their own lunches upstairs in the doctors' dining-room. And perhaps that was what they would have done if they hadn't been stopped in their tracks by a shrill scream from the ward kitchen across the corridor. Jill shot to her feet, overturning her chair, and was inside the kitchen in seconds. There, at the line of work-tops, stood Meg, the younger of the two domestics, staring at her left hand, which she was holding in front of her.

'Kettle spurted. . .boiling!' she gasped as Jill steered her to the sink, where she dashed cold water into the bowl and laid the girl's hand in it.

'It'll take the stinging pain off, Meg. I don't think it's too bad a scald—a nasty thing to happen, though.'

Her reassuring words were drowned by Sir Rodney's bellow of, 'Good prompt action, Staff!' He, Adam Greerson, and Dick were all in the kitchen, Sister as well. It was quite an audience.

Sister went straight to Meg, while Sir Rodney, who liked Jill, proceeded to introduce her to his new registrar. 'Staff has been with us nearly a year now; she's a first-rate nurse.'

Jill turned slowly round, drying her hands, delaying, even now, the exact moment when she would have to look at him. He was taller than her by about half a head, so his face wasn't all that high up. What it registered when their eyes met was a shocked, *My God*! What it actually said, through a mouth that appeared to be difficult to move, was a courteous, 'Good morning, Nurse Arbor,' while his hand clutched hers in a grip of shock, then fell back to his side. He said nothing else, not a thing else, so he wasn't, she realised, going to give her away. She caught Dick's fleeting glance.

'Take Meg to the clinical-room and dress her hand, please, Staff.' Sister spoke with an edge to her voice that broke the little group up. Sir Rodney steered Adam Greerson to the door, Dick followed at their heels, turning round to wink at Jill, while Sister, with consummate skill, managed to squeeze to the front with Sir Rodney and lead the way out to the lifts.

In the clinical-room, ripping open a packet of sofra tulle, Jill could still see Adam Greerson's eyes boring into hers. And he'd limped too. . .when he'd turned to go out of the kitchen he'd limped, very slightly, it was true, but she'd seen it, and felt awful all over again. Still he can't be that bad if he's working, she thought. He might even have put it on for my benefit, for he's that type of man, I'm sure. She washed her hands briskly with hibiscrub, splashing them up to the elbows, wishing that she'd got *him* in the sink, giving him what for.

'The new reg is lovely, isn't he, Staff?' Meg said innocently.

'Oh, absolutely,' Jill said sarcastically, laying the square of dressing over Meg's hand and bandaging it on with feather-light fingers that never put a touch wrong. There was no one quite like Staff Nurse Arbor for dressing a wound. She was a 'natural' and had been praised for it many times before.

'I expect he's married, don't you?' Meg's gooseberry eyes were dreamy.

'Quite possibly, yes. Now does that feel comfortable?' Knotting a sling round Meg's plump neck, Jill threaded her arm in it, completely supporting her hand.

'Yes, thanks, Staff, it's lovely,' Meg sighed, and got up from the chair.

'Go and sit in the rest-room until Sister gets back,' Jill told her, throwing the dressing packets into the bin.

She was completing an accident form in the office when Sister returned to give her a short résumé of the condition of each patient before attending a conference down in Admin Block. This résumé, or hand-over report, took some time to get through.

'Keep a special eye on Mrs Timms,' Sister finished at last. 'She's the strangulated hernia admitted via Cas this morning. Her bowel was found to be gangrenous, so Mr Greerson did a resection. She's on antibiotic therapy, administered through her drip. Here are her notes, with her Casualty card, and the details sent up from Theatre. Oh, and yes, I'm not too happy about Miss Pink and

Mrs Flood—being in neighbouring beds, I mean. I think that was a mistake. We may have to part them; we don't want either of them upset.'

'They're not very compatible, are they?' Jill glanced through the viewing window at the two patients in question, each so different from the other, both of them quarrelsome. Miss Anthea Pink, stowing away her large-print library book, was settling down for a nap, this being the quiet time on the ward. Mrs Flood, kicking off her slippers, was clambering back into bed. She looked elephantine in a white smocked nightdress with big puff sleeves; once between the sheets her shape became one large mound.

'You'd think there was a bed-cradle under there.' Sister followed Jill's gaze. 'No wonder she's got varicositis—it's a wonder her legs survive. Incidentally, I think you'd better send Meg Davies off duty. Give her some tab codeine to take home with her. There always seems to be some sort of accident whenever Meg is around. I find myself holding my breath each time she sets foot in the ward. She'd be better and more safely employed in the kitchens downstairs. Still, as she's fairly new, I suppose we must give her a chance. And, talking of accidents, you'll never believe what happened to Mr Greerson on the car park last night. Someone—a young nurse, he said—ran over his feet on a bike! *On a bike*, in the doctors' car park! She had no right, cycling in there. I don't know if you noticed, but he was limping quite noticeably—he says one of the pedals bashed his ankle, which brought up a bruise. Honestly, Staff, on his first night here. . .have you ever heard the like?'

'It was very bad luck, Jill said, and looked at the opposite wall.

'He made light of it—even joked about it.' Sister got up to go. 'On the whole he seemed to me to be very approachable.'

'Oh, good.' Jill opened the door for her, feeling her face flush warm. Sister Beck noticed and, not unnaturally, assumed that Jill, like all the others, had fallen prey to the new registrar's charms. What it is to be young, she thought, and yet how painful too. Glaring at learner Nurse Sibley, who had burst a laundry bag all over the corridor floor, she went upstairs to lunch.

A bruised ankle wouldn't kill him. Jill sat down at the desk, still feeling warm inside her dress when she thought of what Sister had said. He didn't give me away, and he could have, which was decent of him, I suppose. I also suppose, when I see him, I'm going to have to mention it, even—and she sighed a little—thank him for holding his tongue.

She decided to do a short ward-round before the start of visiting. The Walbrook adhered to the old system of set visiting hours, which meant that everyone knew where they were, including the patients—some of whom wouldn't have wanted relatives and friends homing in on them at any time after lunch. Jill made her way to Miss Pink's bed first, a pallid-looking Miss Pink, who was to undergo a partial gastrectomy next day. She could have no more food by mouth after her supper tonight. Jill explained this to her, and Miss Pink gave a ladylike snort. 'And that will be a relief, Nurse. The food here is a disgrace. That piece of fish I had for lunch was a mass of slimy skin.'

'Oh, dear, I'm sorry.' Jill felt she should sympathise.

'Well, I don't suppose it's *your* fault, is it?' Miss Pink turned her head away, only to meet the beady eye of Mrs Flood in the neighbouring bed.

'She lets things get her down, Staff.' Emily Flood sat up, pulling the cardigan that she wore as a bedjacket round her shoulders like a shawl. 'If she'd had everything taken away, like I did, in the gynae ward last year, then she'd have something to bellyache about.'

'If you'd had everything taken away, as you call it, you wouldn't be in here now,' Miss Pink said disdainfully, 'for there wouldn't be any point.'

'Oh, yes, there would—I'm in for me veins,' Mrs Flood retorted. 'I'm having them stripped and liberated, then I shan't have no more bother.'

'Stripped and *ligated*, Mrs Flood,' smiled Jill. 'It's you who'll be liberated!'

'Well, whatever it is, I'm having it,' Mrs Flood smiled back at her. 'I only wish that smashing young surgeon who come in during lunch would be doing the stripping. Have you seen him, dear?'

'If you mean Mr Greerson, yes, I have.' Jill glanced at Emily's notes, seeing that Jonathan Rule, the vascular surgeon, would be stripping out her vein. She didn't particularly want to think about Adam Greerson any more today.

'So what did you think of him—the new man?' Emily's look was arch, then it sharpened and her mouth gaped. 'Crikey, Staff, he's here. . .he's here *now*. . .he's just come in! He's seen you and he's coming!' Slipping further down the bed, she half closed her eyes, not missing a thing, but adopting an invalid pose.

Jill turned round with fast-beating heart, schooling herself to calm, resisting the urge to smooth down her dress, to put a hand to her hair. He was walking. . .no, strolling up the ward, looking about him as though he owned every bed and its occupant, and was counting them like cash. He also looked, she decided more fairly, as though he was in his right place, which probably meant he was going to be a dab hand at everything. He was only a few yards away now; it was time to smile at him, and be Staff Nurse Arbor, *not* the girl who'd crashed into him in the yard.

'Can I help you, sir?' Her words came out in a kind of bolting rush.

'Yes, I'd like to see Mrs Timms, please.' He was grave and watchful-eyed, and she felt 'on test', sensing his faint distrust of her as a nurse.

'Of course,' she said briefly, handing him the notes, which she'd had under her arm. It was a relief when he looked down at them, when his eyes left her face. 'I was going to see her myself,' she added, 'not that there's been much change. Her temp is still elevated at thirty-eight, her blood-pressure is stable and, as you know, she's on quarter-hourly obs.'

'All right, then, let's go, shall we?' He stood back for her to pass, and lead the way to Mrs Timms' bed, just inside the doors. 'I don't want to disturb her,' he qualified, 'but I'd like to glance at her charts.' He studied them carefully, turning them over against the holding clip. Replacing them just as carefully, he looked down at Mrs Timms. She was sleeping, her thin hair pushed up at the back. A gastric tube trailed her cheek and was taped to her temple; a drip, supported by a pillow, ran into her left arm. 'While peritonitis is still on the cards, continue to aspirate,' he instructed Jill quite unnecessarily as they stood in the centre aisle. 'I may need to increase her potassium and vitamins, but I'll see how she is tomorrow.' He stopped talking and looked at her keenly. 'Sister's off duty, I take it?'

'She's at a conference until four-thirty,' Jill told him pleasantly. 'I'm in charge now until nine-thirty, when the night staff come on.'

'I see.' He was still looking hard at her, and somehow or other he managed to make the two words sound like bad news. The glint in his eye—a very blue eye—laid emphasis to this, and behind the smile she flashed at him she managed not to react.

'Would you like to see any of the other patients, now that you're here, Mr Greerson?' She was forced to step slightly closer to him to allow Rachel Marks to pass by with the trolley of blankets and sheets.

'I don't think so, no.' The top of her head was white starched cap; beneath it her bright hair appeared as a golden rim. 'I'm well aware,' he went on quickly, 'that this is the ward's napping time, but perhaps before I go I could see tomorrow's Theatre list. You'll have a copy somewhere. . .won't you?' He watched her move back from him.

'Of course. . .in the office.' She led the way there, very conscious of him walking close behind her, practically on her heels. Intimidation tactics, she thought— well, they're not going to work, Mr Adam Greerson, sir, for I'm not the timid sort.

Once in the office he closed the door, and before Jill could look for the list he said without warning or preamble, 'I apologise for having thought you a student nurse, when you're very clearly not.'

'I qualified three years ago, but as you've brought it up. . .last night, I mean,' she floundered a little, 'I would like to ask how your ankle is. . .not too painful, I hope?'

'Bruised only—painful, yes.' His narrow-eyed look accused. Jill met it.

'Well, once again, I'm so sorry it happened.' She felt she had to say that, but she found she was unable, in view of his attitude, to eat more humble pie and thank him for not giving her away to Sister Beck.

He sat down suddenly, looking pained, and squawked his chair to the desk. 'Do you want those signed?' He nodded over to the pile of prescriptions sitting under Sister's crocodile paperweight.

'Why, yes, thank you, if you wouldn't mind.' She was surprised at his offering. Prescriptions were usually left to the housemen.

'It'll save Dick a job,' he said. 'He's got Outpatients'

clinic at two. I'm off there myself in a minute. I want to
see how the department is run.'

He was the sort to make changes, Jill thought, searching for the theatre list. It wasn't attached to the board,
where it should have been, so it must be on the desk. He
was still signing, seemingly engrossèd; he was using a
fountain pen—she could hear the faint sound it made as
he scrawled his name over the pad. Oh, where was
it. . .where was that list? Supposing it was lost! What
would he do, what would he say? Oh, where had Sister
put it? She turned over papers to no avail, she upset a
filing tray, then, right on the edge of blind panic, she
saw the list down on the floor.

'Found it?' he asked, and she flushed scarlet, for he
must have seen that she had. He had also seen her
getting flustered, of that she was perfectly sure.

'Yes, it's here.' She thrust it at him, a little too
quickly, perhaps. As she did so their fingers touched,
and she felt the glancing contact like a blaze on her skin,
and swallowed on the fact that as well as everything else
he was arousingly attractive. She gripped her hands
under the desk.

As he laid the list on the blotter and bent his head
over it she studied him carefully, feature by feature,
noting the way his foxy hair sprang away from its
parting, noting the proud straight nose, and the half-
moons of sepia lashes lying so silkily down on his hard-
boned face. He was altering the list, she could see him
doing so. Theatre Sister would go mad! On the other
hand, she might not, for men like Adam Greerson could
get away with murder if they tried. He pushed the list
over the desk to her, thrust back his chair and stood up,
clipping his pen to his coat.

'I'd like Mrs Arnopp put down for nine-thirty, and
Miss Pink after that. In other words, transpose them.
That shouldn't present too many difficulties, should it?'

His eyes met hers with the merest hint of challenge in their sea-blue depths.

'Of course not.' Jill picked up the list as he moved towards the door. She saw his hand depress the handle, then he turned round again.

'But I'll call in at Theatres on my way down, make my peace with Sister Melville. Right, then, Staff, I think that's all. Thank you for your help.'

So we've started, she thought, as surgeon and nurse; perhaps it will be all right. She made her way round the desk, intending to escort him out to the lifts, which was the usual thing to do when senior doctors called. However, guessing her intention, he shook his head. 'I can find my own way,' he said. 'There are enough hanging signs and indicating arrows about, goodness only knows!' And with that he was gone, closing the door with a snappity little click that was every bit as decisive as his voice, and just as dismissive too.

Oh, all right, then, *be* like that! Jill pulled a face at the door, restraining an impulse to whip it open and shout out something rude. He was so unshakeably confident, so with it on all fronts. Anyone would think he bossed the whole show, was the senior consultant himself.

Still, tomorrow he would be the consultant, in all but name, for Tuesday was the day when Sir Rodney Elverton operated at St Mildred's, leaving his next in command to cope with the surgical list at the Walbrook, with the help of his houseman, Dick Lane. So there you are, new registrar, it'll be nose to the scalpel for you up until teatime, and probably later, depending on how nifty you are. You won't have time to come up here and charm the nursing staff senseless, which may be a shocking disappointment for them, but for me it'll be a reprieve.

The visitors were beginning to congregate out in the corridor. Jill could hear the doors at the end thudding open and shut, hear the sound of footsteps, the rustle of paper, the nervous clearing of throats. Soon she would have to hook back the doors and let them go into the ward, but before then she wanted to have a word with Mrs Arnopp, who, due to the altered theatre list, would be first downstairs next day.

She was putting away her knitting as Jill approached her bed. She was a highly strung woman in middle age, who during the past few days had undergone several tiring investigations and tests. Now all she wanted was to get her operation—the removal of her gall-bladder—over and done with, and yet she dreaded it. She confided her fears to Jill, who sat down by her bed. 'My sister-in-law, who came in yesterday, said I'd be in great pain for about a week afterwards. Is that true, Nurse?' she asked.

'No, it's not, Mrs Arnopp.' How some people loved instilling fear into others. 'You'll feel a degree of discomfort, of course,' Jill strove to be honest, 'but we'll give you something to help that, and you'll feel better as each day passes. Your wound will be here,' she indicated Mrs Arnopp's subcostal region, 'and there'll be two tubes coming out of it, one draining into a bag. These will be removed within a week or five days, and then you'll be well on the way to being discharged. I promise you you've nothing to worry about. Your sister-in-law must have been listening to some old wives' tales.'

'Yes, that's what my husband said.' Mrs Arnopp looked relieved. 'He told Margaret off,' she added with a smile that took years off her jaundiced face. 'Thank you for coming to see me, dear; it's made all the difference. Will you be with me when they do it?'

'No, not in the Theatre,' Jill shook her head, 'but I'll be with you in the anaesthetic-room until you're fast asleep. I'll be giving you your pre-med injection here in the ward first. That will make you feel you haven't a care in the world.'

The rustle of the curtains as Jill drew them back

drowned Mrs Arnopp's reply. Leaving her to prepare for her visitors, one of whom would most likely be the morbid Margaret, Jill went to the ward desk and spoke to June Sibley, who was checking intake and output charts. 'You can let the visitors in now,' she said, then moved on down the ward towards the day-room, where two men from Maintenance were waiting by the tree.

'OK to start wiring up?' they asked.

'Yes, please do.' She watched them setting their steps in place, trailing strings of fairy lights. It was a super tree, just brushing the ceiling, its foot in a stout wooden tub. A box of trimmings got out by the nurses stood on a nearby stool. It seemed to Jill that the tree stretched its branches in eager anticipation of being dressed in jewel colours, of being adorned and admired. And it got its wish, for, as the winter afternoon dwindled into early dusk, everyone turned to look at it, glowing in its corner, lending a touch of magic to the ward.

Soon after that the blinds were drawn and the visitors went home. Flowers were put in water, books and magazines were stacked in lockers, nighties and vests were taken out of bags. Teatime came and went. Jill drank her tea in the office, while trying to reassure Mr Timms, who, alarmed at his wife's appearance, had stayed on to ask about her. He felt she might die in the night. 'She looks so ill,' he quavered, but then, so did he, poor man, sitting in the office on a hard-backed chair, with his raincoat on his knees.

'All patients have that ghastly look immediately after surgery. It's due to the anaesthetic drugs,' Jill explained gently. 'Remember, we did advise you not to come in today.'

'I couldn't keep away—I had to come.'

'Yes, I understand that, and I don't blame you for doing so. I'm sure I'd have done the same. But Mrs Timms won't have that pale look tomorrow, and she won't be disorientated.' Jill crossed her fingers as she said this, for she was only too well aware that if Mrs Timms should develop peritonitis, and if it became generalised, her condition would deteriorate markedly, and she could quite easily die. 'She'll be able to talk to you tomorrow,' she added, getting up from her chair.

'Thank you. I hope so—I feel lost without her; it seems so strange at home. It's the first time we've been parted for over thirty years.' After another look at his wife's curtained bed through the viewing window Mr Timms left the office at last, saying that he was obliged.

During the evening one or two patients in dressing-gowns and slippers went into the day-room to watch television. The day-room was shared with Charlestone Ward, which was male surgical, so men and women patients could meet during viewing time. Some of them played cards, or chess, and some of them smoked—on the quiet and against regulations—arousing Sister's ire.

Jill went up to her supper at eight, and Lynn Betts, the staff nurse on Charlestone, stood in for her for the short time it took to bolt down ham and salad, followed by a portion of apple tart. Once back on the ward, she and Nurse Bell prised the television addicts out of the day-room and helped them back to bed. Next they did the medicine round—a slow and meticulous task, as every dose had to be double-checked with the typed drugs list. June Sibley helped with this, flitting from bed to bed with the tablets, or liquid medicine, or both, dispensed from the trolley by Jill. Soon after this the lights were dimmed, and 'Nil by mouth' notices were hung over the beds of patients due for surgery next day. In the ward kitchen late-night drinks were being prepared. The night staff came on duty, and after giving the report Jill collected her cape from the cloakroom and made her way home to Cade House.

Chrissie was back, and came tapping at her door

almost as soon as she got in. The two girls were pleased to see one another.

'The kitchen,' Jill declared, 'hasn't been the same without you!'

'You mean, it's never been so clean,' Chrissie grinned, going over to lie on Jill's divan—a plump, freckle-faced girl in tartan trousers and an Aran jersey that had seen better days.

'Had a good leave?' Jill asked her.

'I've known better.' Chrissie grimaced. 'Edinburgh was like the back of beyond, and I had a lousy journey both ways. I shan't do it again, not just for a week.' She tossed back her mane of red hair. 'If Dad hadn't sent me the fare I wouldn't have tackled it this time, you know. I'm not a great one for family reunions, and all the relatives Ma could drum up came to visit—it was too boring for words! I'm thankful I'm on duty over Christmas and New Year—I couldn't have stood it up there.'

'Never mind,' Jill was sympathetic, 'you're back now,' she said. But she thought, as they sat there exchanging news, how very different they were. She, Jill, was all for going home whenever she could. Even if she'd still had to travel to Cornwall to be with Anna, her grandmother, she would have done it, even for a few days, let alone a week. But with Anna living at Windon, the twenty-five-minute journey down the line from King's Cross was a doddle, no problem at all.

She told Chrissie about Adam and the bike incident, leaving nothing out. Her friend's comment was that Dick was a skunk, but Jill stuck up for him. At least he gave me the ten pounds for the draw tickets.'

'Dirt money!' Chrissie declared, raising one leg in the air, and contemplating her toes. 'Still, I shouldn't worry too much about it—it's something and nothing, you know. Adam Greerson will soon come to realise you're a good senior nurse.'

'I don't much care if he doesn't.'

'Oh, good!' Chrissie gave her a look. 'Well, anyway,' she heaved herself upright, 'what's this bashed-about registrar like?'

'Self-possessed, attractive—sexy, I suppose you'd say.'

'What age?'

Jill considered. 'Mid-thirties, I suppose.'

'Married?'

'I've no idea.' She watched her friend upend herself and go over to the door. 'Actually,' she added, 'it would never surprise me if he's been married and divorced, and is living with someone—he's got that kind of look.'

'You mean dissipated?'

'No, I don't,' Jill strained to be fair, 'but he's got some sharply etched lines on his face, and there's a piercing look to his eye.'

'You've obviously made a study of him.'

'I and the rest of the team, including Sister, who was rose-pink all the time he was on the ward.'

'I can see,' said Chrissie, yawning her way back to her room, 'that I shall have to visit the surgical floor and meet this delectable male. Anyway, 'night, Jill. . .if I don't turn in now I'll fall flat on my face. See you tomorrow.' She flapped her hand and was gone.

Half an hour later, just before she got into bed herself, Jill switched off her light and went to the window, parting the curtains to look down into the hospital yard. Separate buildings stood out like houses—the creeper-clad medical school, the doctors' residence, most of its windows alight like lozenges. Further on were the research laboratories, and further on from those was the start of the car park, alongside which was the boundary

wall and the narrow path where she'd run Adam
Greerson down.

Her gaze passed once more to the residence. Did he
live in, she wondered, or had he got his own place
somewhere in the suburbs? And was he married? It
annoyed her that thoughts of him kept coming into her
mind and clinging there like burrs. She told herself that
this was because of her first crash meeting with him, but
it was more than that, and she knew it, for, like him or
nor, there was something about him that would make
most females turn and stop, and start to wonder. . .

He was a very intriguing man.

CHAPTER TWO

On Tuesday Jill learned that Adam Greerson lived in, while on Wednesday Dick gave her more personal news about him—he believed in passing things on.

'He's not married, Jill, but neither is he going without,' he grinned. 'He's got a very upmarket girlfriend, who has a flat in the Barbican. Apparently she's one of the lady auctioneers at Rothenby's.'

'Been having a heart-to-heart with him, have you?' Jill was filing the notes after Dick's morning round and she turned to look at him.

'Not exactly, no, but I saw them both in the Goldsmith Arms last night. They were in there, having a drink and he introduced me to her. In spite of looking toffee-nosed, she was fairly talkative. . .chatted away all about herself. He's more the strong, silent type.'

'Well, now you can go and add another tendril to the grapevine,' said Jill, mopping up a dribble of milk from the desk. Dick was gulping down a cup of coffee that he'd scrounged from the ward kitchen.

'I like to have a little background knowledge of my betters,' he admitted. 'It gives me a lead into what makes them tick, how they're likely to react. And now, my charming Jillian, I'm off to Charlestone Ward, then it's down to Theatres at half-eleven, where I'm helping with a loop colostomy.' He slammed down his cup, and Jill watched him go.

'What a riveting life you lead,' she called out to his vanishing back, then sat down with her own coffee, her mind on what he'd said.

Adam Greerson had an upmarket girlfriend, did he?

31

Well, that didn't surprise her. Not being married, he'd be bound to have a romantic attachment—he was hardly the sort of man to live like a monk. Rothenby's, the fine-art dealers, were renowned throughout the world, so his girlfriend would have a cracking job. No wonder she could afford to live in the Barbican, which, incidentally, was only a short way from the Walbrook. Jill allowed herself to dwell on this for seconds only, then, abandoning her coffee, she got up and called Nurse Sibley out of the ward.

'Lay up a sterile trolley, June,' she instructed the young girl. 'You can help me with Mrs Timms's dressing.' Part of her job, as senior nurse, was to teach the juniors. There was no time on a busy ward to sit around thinking thoughts that were nothing to do with the patients and their needs, especially when Sister wouldn't be on duty until midday.

At eleven o'clock Joe Buckman, one of the physiotherapy team, arrived to give breathing exercises to Mrs Flixton, who had had a hiatus hernia repaired by Adam the day before. Jill escorted him to the bedside to introduce him to Mrs Flixton, then, leaving them together, she helped two patients on with their dressing-gowns and took them along to the day-room, one on either arm.

'The tree looks a treat!' Mrs Irons wanted to stop and admire it. She had had extensive abdominal surgery, and, although no one had told her, she knew that this coming Christmas would be her last.

'There'll be singing round it on Christmas Eve.' Jill watched her touch one of the tiny silver bells with her thin, veined hand.

'Christmas isn't what it used to be,' Mrs Clay piped up. 'When you're young it's all right, it's magic. Now it's just a chore of cooking the kind of food we can eat every day of the week. Take chicken, for instance. . .'

Mrs Irons blenched. The last thing she wanted to do was talk about food. She didn't even want to think about it, and, knowing this, Jill seated Mrs Clay, who had progressed from chickens to sherry trifle, with her friend Miss Reeve, and took Rose Irons over to the window. Here, with the morning paper and her knitting, she could look out beyond the spires of three City churches to the awesome dome of St Paul's.

'Thank you, dear,' she said, and as Jill lowered her into a chair they exchanged smiles of the conspiratorial kind.

Jill was back in the office, putting away the stores from the pharmacy, when Joe put his dark head round the door again. 'All done for today,' he said, 'but I'll be up the same time tomorrow. Mrs Flixton finds it hard to relax, to put herself into my hands, but it can't be much fun to have to do what causes so much discomfort. If she's to avoid pulmonary collapse, though, she and I are going to have to work together for a few more sessions yet.'

'Her diaphragm has retracted, hasn't it?' Jill had been reading her notes.

'After fundal plication that happens,' Joe said, just as Sister arrived, throwing her cape off matador-fashion and dropping it on to a chair. She greeted Joe with enthusiasm.

'Just the man I wanted to see! Mr Greerson would like Mrs Devonshire started on abdominal exercises as from tomorrow afternoon. She's the peritonitis in bed number ten—now doing very well. She's on normal feeding. . .' The rest of her sentence was lost on Jill, as she slipped from the office and made her way into the ward.

By the time Joe had gone back to the department of physical medicine the luncheon trolleys had arrived in the ward, and Sister had come out of the office to deal with the serving, helped by the learner nurse. Jill was called to take over, however, when Sister was called to the phone. Back she came, bristling a little, with the news that a bed had to be got ready for an emergency admission—an RTA victim with a ruptured spleen, who was already in Theatre.

'She's a twenty-one-year-old girl,' said Sister. 'Adam Greerson is operating. She's likely to be coming up here from Recovery in about two hours.'

'We've no bed free, Sister.' Jill was serving out a portion of mince and potato.

'I'm well aware of that.' Sister pushed in front and took full charge of the trolley again. 'Number two sideward is vacant, though, so we'll move Mrs Flood in there. That will help us in two ways—give us a free bed in here, and little Miss Pink the peace and quiet she needs. I've no notes for the splenectomy, but I'm told that A and E have informed her parents, who are on their way here. She's Ruth Gardner, by the way.'

She'll be the youngest in the ward, thought Jill as she applied a bandage, of the elastic support variety, to Mrs Flood's leg.

'Why it is me who 'as to be moved?' Emily looked disgruntled.

'Because. . .' Jill helped her down from the bed and took her arm '. . .you're about the only patient not on a drip or drain.' This wasn't strictly true, and she knew it, but there were times when little lies had to be told to keep the peace, or to save a patient stress.

'I thought p'raps she'd been complaining about me.' Emily nodded towards Miss Pink, who had her eyes closed, probably with intent.

'By not so much as a word,' replied Jill. 'What made you think she had?'

'Well, she's toffee-nosed, isn't she? Thinks she's a cut above. What I say is, when you come into 'ospital you 'ave to learn to mix. Still, a room of my own will be nice—I can get up to all sorts of tricks.'

'Such as?' Jill enquired, and the two of them were laughing, when they saw a tall figure in Theatre greens coming towards them from the end of the corridor, making plopping sounds in his white boots. It was Adam Greerson. Jill felt herself tense, felt her neck going stiff. He was getting nearer, looming larger, seeming to fill her vision. He must have come straight up from Theatre, so the splenectomy patient had either died on the table, or was off it and out, being looked after and stabilised in the recovery-room. These happenings, or possible happenings, flew into Jill's mind in the few seconds it took for him to draw level with them.

'Sister on duty?' He scarcely halted, and she could smell anaesthetic gas.

'In the ward, serving lunches. Would you like me——?'

'No, you carry on.' He glanced through the porthole doors, then swept through them, while Emily sighed, breathing in the theatre odour with a look of bliss on her face.

'Pity he was in such an 'urry.' She turned to look after him, but the ward doors had swung to behind him, and all she could see through the portholes was the back of his head moving across the ward. 'Macho, isn't he?' She wheezed a little. 'Even in that green thing.'

'I suppose he is,' Jill agreed, not sure that 'macho' described him. He was all male, certainly, but the single word 'macho' conjured up a boastful type of man. And, to be fair, I don't think he's boastful, just naturally confident, she thought to herself, trying to ignore the drumming in her ears, which was her stupid and startled heart going into top gear.

Emily was thrilled when she saw the side-ward. 'It's like going private, dear!' She stared round at its pale blue walls and new white paint. The bed had been warmed, and she sighed with pleasure as Jill helped her into it. 'But I'll be home for Christmas, won't I?' she enquired anxiously.

'Heavens, yes,' Jill assured her, 'there are still thirteen days to go.' As she tucked Emily up she saw Adam pass the open doorway. The plopping of his boots was regular and even—he no longer limped, and thank heaven for that! His ankle must be better, so she could stop feeling conscience-stricken. He must be going back to Theatres. Was the splenectomy girl all right? It would be awful for him, terrible for him, to lose a patient in his first week. Ruth Gardner was only twenty-one—still, that might be in her favour. 'Shall I turn on your radio for you?' she asked Emily Flood.

'Yes, if you like, dear.' Emily was pleased to see that all her belongings were in the locker at the side of the bed, including her tin of sweets. 'Leave the door open when you go out; then I can see what's going on.'

'We never shut patients up,' Jill told her, fixing her head-piece and showing her where the bell-push was, should she need to summon a nurse.

Leaving her tuned in to Radio Two, she went into the main ward, where she found Nurses Bell and Sibley making up the vacated bed. So, she thought, Ruth Gardner has survived—thank goodness for that! She watched the two girls making a pack of the top clothes, laying it ready at the foot of the bed, shaking pillows into cases, tucking a drawsheet in place. A stand for transfusion equipment stood on the right-hand side, and there was a bowl and wipes on the locker, together with a sphyg, and an inflatable cuff; two types of mask hung by the oxygen point.

'The patient is still in Recovery, Staff.' Sister came to Jill's side. 'And those masks aren't going to do, I'm afraid. If she needs oxygen Mr Greerson wants it administered through a bag-mask, the lightweight disposable kind. I think you'll find some in the clinical-room; if not we'll have to borrow from Charlestone, just for this afternoon.'

Jill went to look, and found what was needed. Now surely that was the lot. Soon after the afternoon visitors filed into the ward. They were still there when Ruth Gardner was brought up from Recovery. The little procession—the patient on the trolley, a porter at each end, the recovery-room nurse on the right-hand side, holding a blood bottle high—caused a ripple of ghoulish fascination to run through the ward. One or two visitors actually stood up to get a better view as the trolley was eased alongside the bed, next to a dozing Miss Pink.

Ruth mumbled unintelligibly as the porters lifted her, the theatre canvas was slipped from beneath her and the bedclothes unfolded on top. A glance at the notes told Jill that her spleen had been removed through a left subcostal incision, and that the wound was being drained. She was on quarter-hourly observations, and Nurse Marks had been deployed to record these and to report any significant change.

No sooner had the last of the visitors gone than Sir Rodney Elverton and Adam strolled in, wanting to do a round. Jill hastily collected all the case-notes they would need, while Sister stood over her, voicing her annoyance in no uncertain terms. 'They don't have to ask my permission to come, but you'd think they'd have the nous or common courtesy to give us at least five minutes' warning!' Thrusting the trolley of notes before her, she joined the two surgeons by the Christmas tree, bending her face in a smile.

In the end only six patients were seen—the day before's post-ops—then Sir Rodney sloped off, head down low, looking at his feet. This was the way he

always walked, as though hoping that he might find
something of interest, or value, on the ground.

Adam was with Sister at the ward desk; Jill could see
them poring over someone's X-ray films, probably Mrs
Arnopp's. Meg Davies came in with a vase of flowers in
her uninjured hand, carrying it tilted, carrying it care-
lessly, as she stared about the ward. Jill was at Mrs
Flixton's bed, tidying her locker. She saw Meg and held
her breath—the girl looked so unaware, so dreamy, so
likely to spill water all over the floor. Meg was clumsy
even with two good hands, and with one in bandages she
was positively dangerous; she should never have been in
the ward. But it was one of those times, Jill decided,
when to call out a warning might bring about the very
disaster she was hoping to avoid. It happened, though;
it happened anyway. . .out of Meg's hand slid the vase,
straight through her fingers, as though she'd forgotton
to maintain a grip. It hit the floor with a splintering
crash—it almost seemed to explode. Shards of glass flew
in all directions and water streamed over the floor, while
the flowers—tawny hothouse chrysanthemums brought
in for Mrs Devonshire—lay in a heap, their heads as
drenched as their stalks.

Meg stepped back from them, staring, as though they
were nothing to do with her. One or two patients gave
startled cries; others craned their necks to see. Up at the
far end of the ward Adam and Sister Beck, seeing that
Jill was on the scene, turned back to their X-ray films.
Jill, vexed but trying to hide it, told June Sibley to clear
up the mess. 'But don't, Nurse, be tempted to touch any
of the glass with your hands. Sweep it up, every single
fragment, then dry the floor thoroughly. And no, I'm
sorry,' she looked at Meg, 'I don't want you helping. I'd
rather you stayed in the kitchen and kept there. The
flowers are the nurses' job.'

'She knows that, I've told her often enough.' Sister

appeared at Jill's side, while Adam—Jill glanced round—was at Mrs Arnopp's bed.

'It wasn't my fault.' Meg sounded aggrieved, and she omitted to say she was sorry. 'The vase was all wet and I couldn't hold it. . .it shouldn't have been like that,' she finished belligerently, then flounced off to the kitchen, where she told Claire Ford, the other domestic, that Sister Beck had a down on her, and Nurse Arbor was as bad.

Sister went back to join Adam, June Sibley swept up the glass, and Mrs Timms called out to Jill, who crossed over to her bed. She wanted to show her a photograph of her grandson that her husband had brought in. Jill was admiring it, but keeping an eye on the floor situation. She saw June coming in with a drying cloth, but also, at the same moment, saw Sister making tracks for the corridor, which inevitably meant that she was going to step on that damp patch. . .

'Sister. . .the floor. . .watch out!' The warning was quick, and came in time, but Sister didn't heed it, just flapped a hand at Jill. Perhaps she thought she bore a charmed life, that nothing could happen to her. But happen it did. Her heel skidded, the other followed suit, she heard her own cry, had a split-second's view of the ward turning upside-down, and then she was flat on her back on the vinyl, too stunned to feel any pain.

When the pain came it was in her arms, but by then Jill was beside her, carefully and gently sitting her up, helped by Adam. Their eyes met over her head, then Sister vomited into a bowl hastily brought by a shocked Nurse Bell, while Nurse Sibley simply stood there, looking frightened to death with the drying cloth still in her hands.

Jill wiped Sister's face. 'You'll feel better presently.'

'I've broken my wrist.' Sister tried to get up, but Adam restrained her.

'Stay there, just as you are, Sister. Get a chair,' he barked at Nurse Bell. 'No, not one of those. . .' he looked exasperated as she brought one from Mrs Timms's bed '. . .a *wheelchair*,' he emphasised, and he hadn't, Jill realised, very much patience to spare for staff who weren't quick on the draw. His face, however, bore no irritation as he turned it to Sister. 'I'm very much afraid,' he said, moving her other arm, 'that you've fractured *both* wrists—you don't do things by halves. We'll have to get you down to Casualty.' He looked across at Jill, who was removing Sister's wedding-ring, knowing that in a matter of half an hour or so her fingers would start to swell.

'Couldn't someone have warned her?' he asked quietly. Jill was certain that he meant her.

'I *was* warned.' Sister's fall hadn't affected her ears. 'Staff Nurse called out, I heard her, but the phone was ringing out in my office. I suppose I just thought. . .' Her voice trailed off as the wheelchair arrived, and Adam and Jill helped her up into it. 'There's nothing wrong with my legs—I can walk,' she protested.

'Not after a fall like that, you can't.' It was Jill who spoke this time, forestalling Adam, who, it seemed to her, wanted to boss the whole show. Each of Sister's arms was laid on each of the wheelchair arms.

'Better than slings till you're plastered,' Adam smiled down at her. She smiled back, even laughed, but Jill didn't, she was too upset. Perhaps she should have done more than just call out a warning to Sister; perhaps she should have *moved* and prevented her, flapped her arms about, or engaged her in a rugger tackle. She was being absurd, she knew that. She had done all she could, but *he* didn't think so. She looked balefully at Adam, who was moving behind the wheelchair. She was astonished when he started to push it, and looked at him, eyebrows raised.

'I'll take her. . . I'll take Sister down to Casualty,' she said.

'I think not. . .you're needed here.' His eyes swept the ward, which was full of interested and agape patients, all straining to see and hear exactly what was going on. 'You'll need to calm this lot down.'

'Mr Greerson's right, Jill. You stay here,' Sister backed him up. 'And ring Miss Cooper, the SNO, for you're going to need extra help.' For the first time Jean Beck was beginning to realise what two fractured wrists would mean. She would be in a Colles' forearm plaster— *two* of them, moreover—for four to six weeks, and she wouldn't be able, wouldn't be *allowed* to do her proper job for maybe another month after the plaster was off. And that was if everything went right, if there were no complications. Her head whirled as she tried to sort out what was to be done, here on the ward, and also how she would manage at home.

Once the little cortège had left Jill sprang into action, making sure that the floor was safe first of all, then dealing with the patients, calming them down, satisfying their curiosity. . .Yes, Sister slipped up. . .No, we don't know what will happen yet. . .Yes, I'm sure she'll be all right soon. . .No, she hasn't broken her leg. In the middle of it all the Gardners arrived, wanting to see their daughter. Jill put them in the waiting-room, supplied them with tea, explained that Mr Greerson wanted to see them, and that he wouldn't be very long. In the office she rang down to Casualty, and was told he was on his way up. She rang Miss Cooper, the senior nursing officer, who also arrived and asked her to stay on duty till the night staff took over. 'I'm sorry about the double shift, but we'll sort something out tomorrow.' Off went Miss Cooper to see Sister, who had just come out of X-Ray. The boy with the evening newspapers dumped them down on the floor, and Meg Davies came in with a cup of tea, spilling into the saucer, to tell Jill she was fed up with working with nurses, and intended to apply for a transfer to the staff canteen as soon as possible.

Just at that moment Jill couldn't have cared less if she'd been going to work on Mars, but she was glad of the tea, slop and all, and was just finishing it when she saw Adam passing the doorway with the Gardners, and rose to accompany them, only to have him flap her down from the ward side of the window.

'I can manage,' he mimed, and she sat down again, not minding too much, for she'd still got the daily nursing report to complete for the SNO, not to mention Sister's accident form and requisitions for supplies, and in another half-hour it would be ward suppers, then evening visitors, then supper for herself, because even she had to eat.

She was about to ring down to A and E to ask how Sister was when she saw Adam coming out of the ward, having left the Gardners at Ruth's bedside. 'I've told them ten minutes, no longer,' he said. 'She's barely awake, but she knew them, which pleased them.' He sat down on the desk. 'Sister, by the way, is out of Minor Ops and is in the plaster-room. X-ray showed a stable fracture of her right wrist, an unstable one of the left. She'll stay in the accident ward overnight. Her husband has been informed and is on his way here—I gather they live out Hendon way.'

'Yes, they do. He—Mr Beck—retired last year.'

'So I gather. Well, at least he'll be able to look after her at home. She'll be off work, you know, for two months at least—more like three, I'd say.'

'I realise that, and I'm sure she does, and I'm equally sure that the SNO will find a replacement for whatever time is involved.' Adam looked dubious, or she thought he did, and also thought she knew why, but even she was surprised to hear herself saying pointedly, 'But please don't worry, it's highly unlikely to be me. Miss Cooper will almost certainly contact the agency.'

'Oh, good!' His relief was patent, and perhaps if Jill hadn't been quite so exhausted by the events of the past few hours she wouldn't have felt so angered by his lack of faith in her. As it was, she had to use all her control not to be openly rude. And when he got up to go, and she saw that he'd sat in some of Meg's slopped-over tea, she didn't bother to tell him, just let him go off with a very unpleasant-looking pale brown stain on the back of his clean white coat.

CHAPTER THREE

DESPITE what she'd said to Adam, Jill wasn't too surprised to be summoned to Miss Cooper's office next morning and asked if she would like to take over Sister Beck's job for the next eight to ten weeks.

'You see, we feel, Nurse Arbor,' Miss Cooper got up to close the casement window, 'that you're the obvious choice; you know the ward—you've had charge of it before, during Sister's periods of leave and weekends, that kind of thing. What I propose to do—that is, if you're willing to take the job on—is to appoint you as acting sister and recruit a qualified nurse from the agency to make up the nursing team. I've already been in touch with them, and they have a Nurse Catling, who could be available to start with us on the lates shift today. We've had her before—she was with us in the summer on the orthopaedic wards. She'd fit in with you; she's a pleasant woman. So what do you say?' Her look was enquiring, but no more than that. There was no question of 'must'. Jill knew she could refuse if she liked, but how short-sighted that would be. One day she hoped to be a sister—or ward manager—in her own right, and this was her chance to prove herself, to show what she could do. Without hesitation, therefore, she agreed with Miss Cooper's plan, but had one or two qualms even so, for managing the ward for eight or ten weeks was a far cry indeed from merely filling in over holiday periods, or sick leave, or days off.

'And, needless to say,' Miss Cooper was reaching for her phone, 'Sister Jeeves from Charlestone Ward will always be ready with help if you need it. Now don't forget to look in on Sister Beck on your way up. She's going home immediately after breakfast; her husband is fetching her.'

Thus dismissed, Jill made her way along to the observation ward. Sister was up and dressed in her uniform—the only clothes she had with her. She looked wan and worried, for pain very often had that effect. The observation ward was primarily for one-night stays, and there was no other patient in the little bay of six beds that led off from the cubicles. Sister was spooning up cereal and talking to Casualty Sister, who looked at her watch and took her leave when she saw Jill approach.

'Have you seen Miss Cooper?' asked Jean Beck before Jill could speak.

'Yes, I've just come from Admin, and I've agreed to take over in your absence, Sister. I'll do my best to run things exactly the same.'

'You're the girl for the job—I told Miss Cooper that last night.' Sister pushed her cereal bowl away, her plaster knocking against the side of the locker as she did so; she raised her white-encased arms. 'Look at these. . .I ask you. . .they feel like ton weights. Wouldn't you think that by now medical science would have devised a better way of splinting broken bones? Plaster. . .it's archaic! I can't even dress myself properly. Yes, all right, I know what you're going to say—I'm supposed to move them about. All the same, it's frustrating.'

'And painful,' Jill sympathised.

'At this early stage, yes, but I've got some pain-killing tabs to take home with me. I don't intend to suffer needlessly.' She moved her arms back to her lap.

'You'll be very much missed on the ward.' Jill knew this to be true.

'So will you, if you don't get back to it,' Jean Beck

said sharply as frustration at her disablement gnawed at her again.

Jill was just getting up to go when Adam and Dick Lane made their appearance, and she stood back while greetings were exchanged.

'Meet my replacement.' Jean Beck looked towards her and smiled. Dick was quick to say he was pleased but Adam's reaction was slower.

He was most likely, Jill thought, too stunned to utter, but eventually he turned, and said affably enough, 'Then I'm sure we shall be in very capable hands.' It was a pity that he couldn't smile as well, to lend weight to his words, but he had at least gone through the motions, and she couldn't expect more than that.

She didn't see him again until next day, Friday afternoon, and by then she was feeling that she had been acting sister for years. She was enjoying it, though, and coping well, for there'd been no snide remarks. Everyone rallied round her, and all the nurses were pleased. Sister Jeeves, from Charlestone, had reaffirmed her willingness to help, should she run into difficulties, and Irene Catling, who'd arrived for duty at twelve noon the day before, had quickly settled into her role of senior staff. As Miss Cooper had predicted, Jill liked her, recognising that she could be left in charge when she, Jill, was off, which made for peace of mind. Jill was, therefore, sticking to the duty roster got out by Sister Beck the week before, and was taking her weekend off as planned.

When Adam made his way down the corridor *en route* for the ward she was in one of the pay-phones, talking to her grandmother, who had just rung through. Anna Stevens had telephoned to tell her that the trains from King's Cross down to Bexford and beyond were all going slow, because of some dispute with the guards. 'Look, darling, get a taxi,' she said. 'I'll stand the expense. It'll be absolute bedlam on the trains, and after a day on the ward you can well do without that, I'm sure, and all the buses will be packed.'

'All right, Anna; thanks, I'll do that,' Jill agreed at once, on the itch to get back to the office because she'd seen Adam passing the phone. 'See you later—I've got loads to tell you. 'Bye, then, for now.' She left the booth, and, willing herself not to scuttle *too* much, joined Adam in the office. He was at the filing cabinet, and his back view looked impatient. She apologised at once. 'I'm sorry to have kept you waiting, but I had an outside call.'

'Boyfriend?' He turned round, raising a quizzical brow.

'Grandmother.' She was equally short.

'Not an SOS, I hope?' His face changed slightly.

'Oh, there's nothing wrong,' she said. 'She was ringing to tell me there's trouble on the railway from King's Cross down into Herts. I'm going home for the weekend, you see. It's a nuisance, but there it is.'

'Where's home, where do you live?' He lodged on the edge of the desk.

'At Windon, just outside Bexford, but I shall get a taxi,' she said grandly, 'and do it the easy way. Now, how can I help you, Mr Greerson? Were you wanting to see Miss Pink?' she added as she saw the notes in his hand.

'Yes, I would like to see her.' He slipped down from the desk, opened the notes at the treatment section, and looked at Miss Pink's drugs.

'She's made rapid strides since Thursday,' Jill said as they walked through into the ward, 'and she tells me she has a sister who can look after her at home.'

'Couldn't be better, and that will free a bed for a vagotomy patient who I know Sir Rodney is anxious to admit,' Adam said, standing aside to allow Jill to precede him into the ward.

He saw Mrs Arnopp as well as Miss Pink, studied Ruth Gardner's charts, then turned to the office and didn't, for once, seem to want to hurry away. 'I'm glad Miss Cooper kept to her word and got you an agency nurse. At least you can stick to your off-duty times, and not be worked to death.'

Jill glanced at him quickly, more than a little surprised at his concern. 'Nurse Catling has had a good deal more experience than me, she said.

'She's older than you so has had a head start.' He made for the door, stood there motionless for a second, then turned and faced her again. 'I could give you a lift home, if that would help,' he said offhandedly. 'I'm going to Bexford myself. . .spending the weekend with my mother. What time does your shift finish?'

'At. . .half-four.' She stared at him.

'Which is when I planned to leave.'

'But won't it. . .' Jill was taken aback and could hardly enunciate the words '. . .but won't it be a nuisance, take you out of your way?'

'I shouldn't think so. I have to pass through Windon in order to get to Bexford.' He half smiled, but didn't press her, just waited for her answer, one hand on the door-jamb, the other on his hip.

'Well, then, thank you. . .thank you very much.' Jill was fast recovering her poise. 'It would be a help, a great help, so I'll take you up on it.'

'Splendid!' His smile broadened. 'I'll meet you down in the hall at a quarter to five. Can you manage that, do you think?'

She said that she could, and as he went off she sat down in the nearest chair and took several deep, steadying breaths. Never let it be said, she told herself, that the leopard can't change his spots. Adam Greerson has not only changed his, but he's practically blotted them out!

His car, a dark red Lotus, was the last word in luxury. Even the seatbelt had an extra-comfortable feeling about it, Jill thought an hour later as they headed out of town. The Friday evening traffic made conversation difficult, but he had switched the radio on and the tinkling strains of Handel's *Water Music* drifted about their ears.

Driving home with him, Jill decided, no longer seemed at all strange, no longer extraordinary, just perfectly natural. A glance at him out of the corner of her eye showed him to be a relaxed driver, yet watchful behind the wheel. His hair looked almost black in the dark, nearly matching his jacket—a zipped-up one of the anorak type, which he was wearing over his suit. His surgeon's hands, broad and strong, rested easily on the wheel. His chin was raised, showing his jaw and the rounded start of his throat. He was all male, powerful, exciting. Disturbing, amatory thoughts rose unbidden to Jill's mind, making her curl her toes. Quickly she looked away, and out of the window, staring at buildings, willing those thoughts away.

Once they were past Mill Hill junction and heading for Windon Park the traffic was a little lighter, and, turning the radio down, Adam asked her what she was going to do with herself over the weekend.

'I shall take my cue from Anna, my grandmother,' she said. 'She may have got something special laid on, or she may be busy writing. She's Anna Stevens, the novelist— she writes family sagas. You may have seen her books in the shops. . .she's very well known.'

'I certainly *have* seen her books in the shops!' She had caught his interest now; she could hear it in the lift of his voice. 'She's a best-selling novelist!'

'Yes.' Jill laughed out loud, pleased at the impact she'd made.

'My mother is one of her fans. She's read all her

books, and has heard her speak at the Bexford Assembly Rooms!' He still sounded amazed.

'She gives talks all over the place. She's even given one in Ireland.'

'You must be tremendously proud of her.'

'Couldn't be more so. I drop her name into conversations whenever I can. She's not a scrap puffed-up, she's very modest, very much feet-on-the-ground.'

'She's your mother's mother, is she. . . Anna Stevens is her real name?'

'Yes, it's her real name,' and now Jill was holding her breath, hoping that he wouldn't go on and ask about her parents. Quickly she told him a little more about Anna— how hard she worked, and what long hours, and how tired she often got. After that they seemed to pass naturally on to the subject of their own work. He asked her where she had done her training and she answered that readily enough.

'At Bexford General, then I staffed there for two years till I came to the Walbrook. I have a special affection for the General—I don't know why.'

'Perhaps because you had a retinue of boyfriends there.' His statement was partly a question.

'I had my share,' she told him lightly, 'and there's safety in numbers.'

'So you want to be safe?' The bus they were passing streamed shadows on to Jill's face.

'I certainly don't want to be *unsafe*,' was her honest and swift reply.

He made no attempt to cap it, but went on to tell her about his student days at Seftonbridge, and the posts he had filled at St Luke's. He said nothing about his upmarket girlfriend, but then, why should he? Jill reasoned, annoyed with herself for feeling curious.

He took the right-hand fork at the aircraft factory, and soon they were driving down the long hill towards the little town of Windon Park. The shops were still open and awash with light as they drove through the High Street. Glittering bowler-hatted snowmen, sack-laden Father Christmases, trees and trees and still more trees could be seen in most of the windows. Coloured streamers hung from doorways, and banners could be glimpsed inside the main supermarket, with the message 'Merry Christmas', repeating itself across the ceiling from toiletries to cheese.

'Are you on duty over Christmas?' Adam braked at the lights.

Jill averted her eyes from the row of naked birds hung up in the butcher's. Scarcely a pretty sight, she thought as she turned and said, 'Yes, I'm on duty all over Christmas, but off for New Year. How about you?'

'Off on Christmas Day only,' he said, then asked her to give him directions. 'I don't know Windon all that well. Where do I go from here?'

She told him, adding that one of the Walbrook's doctors—Dr Charles Farne—lived at Windon. 'He's one of the nice ones,' she said.

'Oh, I see, we've got nasty ones too, have we?'

She laughed and let that pass. 'Our house is called Homewood—you need to slow now, it's the third one on the right.'

He found it without any difficulty—a red-brick house with a steeply pitched roof, lanky chimneys and attractive leaded windows. There was a circular drive, and as he steered the car over the gravel to the front door he could smell cypresses and see the outline of a bird-table in the centre of one of the lawns.

Jill was undoing her seatbelt and preparing to get out. Should she or should she not ask him in? It wouldn't seem very polite just to get out and go, would it? So, as the car ground to a halt, she took her courage in both hands. 'Would you like to come in,' she said, 'and meet Anna? I know she'd be very pleased.'

'Thank you, yes, I'd love to,' he said, just as the porch light snapped on and a woman called out from the top of the steps, while a small yapping dog scattered the gravel as it tore towards the car.

'Jill, I've got the fare here!' The woman's voice rose up. As she descended the steps Adam saw her more plainly—a small, slight figure, soft hair clouding her face, the wind blowing her skirt, which was full and dark, back from her legs. She walked carefully over the stones.

'Anna!' Jill went forward and kissed her. 'This isn't a taxi, darling.'

'So I see, now I'm nearer to it.' Anna Stevens eyed the Lotus with considerable respect, then looked enquiringly at Adam, who stood waiting to be introduced.

'This is Mr Greerson,' Jill said quickly. 'He gave me a lift. He. . .his mother lives at Bexford. Mr Greerson, meet my grandmother, Anna Stevens.' Having got that over, she watched them shake hands, and tried to quieten the little dog, whose yaps had turned to growls.

'Well, let's go in, out of this wind, for heaven's sake!' Anna scooped up her dog and led the way into the house. 'His name's Barney, and if you could bear to speak to him, he'll stop snarling at you,' she said to Adam, who promptly stepped forward and patted the little dog's head.

'Good evening, Barney,' he said solemnly, and instantly the growls gave way to small sounds of canine approval and much wagging of tail.

They all laughed. 'What breed is he?' asked Adam. 'He's small for a Jack Russell.'

'He's a hunt terrier,' Anna supplied. By this time they were in the main sitting-room, with its closed curtains and glowing coal fire. Adam gained a swift impression of low comfortable chairs, of the gleam of dark wood under shaded lights, of pictures on pale walls, of a soft-pile carpet under his feet. Once seated he was offered sherry. 'As I'm driving, half a glass,' he said a little ruefully, leaning back to drink it, jacket unzipped, legs crossed, Barney sniffing at his shoes. 'What a charming room, Mrs Stevens.' And a charming hostess to boot, he thought as he watched her handing Jill her sherry and sitting down to drink her own.

Anna smiled at him over her glass. 'I like the whole house,' she said. 'It suits me perfectly.'

'Have you lived here long?'

'Just over two years. I came here from Fowey, Cornwall. I wanted to be nearer Jill, and also closer to London. It's convenient to have only a thirty-minute journey when I need to get up to town.'

'I can see that,' Adam said, looking from her to Jill. The youth fairy must have been at both their christenings, he thought. Anna Stevens, who had to be in her sixties, looked at least ten years younger, while Jill could have passed for eighteen. . .hadn't he taken her for exactly that age at their first encounter nearly a week ago? There was no family likeness, he decided, except for the eyes. They both had light brown wide-spaced eyes—Anna Stevens's matching her hair, Jill's contrasting more strikingly with her pale gold fringe.

She was sitting forward in her chair, the narrow skirt of her uniform dress doing its best to ride up over her knees. Aware of his gaze, she tugged it down, while telling Anna that Mrs Greerson, Adam's mother, was one of her fans.

'She certainly is,' Adam confirmed, 'and she once heard you speak—give a talk to the Women's Institute— at the Bexford Assembly Rooms. She'd only just joined then, hadn't been living in Hertfordshire long.'

'I believe it was in the summer.' Anna was thinking

back, her slim brows drawing together, then quickly clearing again. 'Oh, yes, of course, I remember now, a Mrs Greerson gave the vote of thanks.'

'That would be Ma,' Adam smiled, 'that's very much her scene. She's what you might call a committee lady, loves organising things.'

'She was very kind, praised my books, and the talk I'd given. I felt she went rather over the top, for I'm not that brilliant.' Anna bent and lifted a scrabbling Barney on to her lap.

Adam and Jill exchanged glances. I told you she was modest, Jill's smile said, while Adam, reading it aright, smiled back at her, unable to stop himself.

After that the conversation between the three of them moved on to more general things, like the coming of Christmas, the way it seemed to start earlier each year, the amount people spent on presents, and the rising cost of everything in the shops. The crime wave was touched upon, Anna mentioning that a house at the top of Longcroft Road had been burgled a few nights ago. 'I'm having an alarm system installed after Christmas,' she said. 'It seems to me that women on their own can't be too careful.'

Adam agreed with her, then began to make movements to go. 'I must leave you ladies in peace and get home. I've so much enjoyed meeting you,' he said to Anna as they all got up.

'It was kind of you to bring Jill home.' Anna noticed him glancing at a photograph of Jill with her parents—a studio photograph in a silver frame that stood on the mantelshelf. It had been taken the year before Jill had left school. He made no comment on it, and, when Jill returned after seeing him off, Anna asked if she had told him about her parents.

'We're not really on those kind of terms, Anna—I

mean, not the kind of terms to make swapping family histories easy, so no, I haven't,' she said.

'He's an attractive man—the hero type.' Anna looked reflective.

'I agree, he is.' Jill was taking the glasses into the kitchen, 'but he's not always as affable as he was this evening,' she said over her shoulder. 'He can be very crushing. . .very down-putting, and I'm not altogether sure if he approves of my being acting sister. He thinks I'm too young. . .and frivolous.' She told her grandmother about the bike incident.

'He's too big a man to hold that against you for very long,' said Anna. Then, as they reached the kitchen and began preparations for their meal, she told Jill that she would have to work over the weekend. 'I'm at a critical stage in my novel, Jilly, which isn't much fun for you, but I'll try my best to get forward so that we can have Sunday to ourselves.'

'Oh, don't worry, I don't mind.' Jill turned round from the sink. 'I'll cook the meals and see to the shopping—be a joy to have around!'

'You always are,' Anna laughed, but still looked worried. 'And there's Barney,' she said. 'I've made an appointment for him to have his nails clipped tomorrow morning. He needs his anal gland emptied too. Could you bear to take him? You can have the car, obviously, and Clive will be pleased. He was asking about you the other day. I said you'd be home this weekend.'

'Of course I'll take Barney, and it'll be great to see Clive,' Jill assured her, her thoughts turning from Adam to Clive as though stretching themselves in relief.

There was nothing even remotely complicated about Clive Barnett. He was the junior partner in Fentons— the local veterinary group. Three and a half years ago Jill had been going to marry him. He had asked her at the time of her parents' death, and she'd accepted at once, in the firm belief that he could make her happy, and that she could return his love. But as time went on they had discovered that what they felt wasn't strong enough to last a lifetime, there was little to build on, and so they had decided to part. Now they met as friends, just very occasionally, usually in the company of others. And in that Jill felt they were lucky, for broken engagements often brought the kind of unhappiness that lasted for years afterwards,

There were three people in the waiting-room when she got to the surgery next morning. There was a young man in denim dungarees with a greyhound between his knees, and a little boy sitting with a box on his lap, most likely containing a gerbil or a rabbit, thought Jill, giving her name at the desk. On the chair nearest the outside door sat an elderly woman in tweeds—tweed hat, coat and skirt, expensive leather boots. She was annoyed at being kept waiting. 'My appointment was for ten o'clock, and it's already a quarter past,' she said, making sure the receptionist heard.

'Mr Barnett has to deal with an emergency, and it's put his list out.' The receptionist—a young Saturday girl— went red, and scratched her neck.

'That sometimes happens,' Jill said pleasantly, smiling over at her in an attempt to lighten the atmosphere, which wasn't the comfortable sort.

Against the side of the tweed woman's boot stood a wicker cat-carrying basket. Through its mesh window Jill could see a movement of white fur. Picking up Barney for absolute safety, she seated herself on the other side of the little room, holding him on her knee. He knew what was inside that wicker basket, for he was growling deep in his throat, quivering his nose and leaning forward as far as he could on Jill's lap. He gave a short but ear-splitting bark, and everyone in the room jumped, even the young receptionist, who was well used to yapping dogs. The cat basket did a backward shunt, moving at least six inches.

'You're terrorising Seamus!' the tweed woman snapped, glaring at Jill as though she were the culprit and had done the barking herself.

'I'm so sorry, but Barney doesn't like cats.' Jill tucked him under her arm and moved over to the floor-length window, in the hope of diverting him by getting him interested in what was happening outside.

'They're such snappy little dogs, Jack Russells. . .pretty enough, I agree, but not to be trusted.' The tweed woman moved the basket on to her knees.

'Actually Barney's quite gentle in all other respects.' It was necessary to defend him, Jill thought, especially as he'd decided to behave himself and was watching the traffic waiting to get through the lights. On the opposite side of the busy road which led down into the High Street was a travel agent's, and next to that a tele-radio shop. From the latter Christmas music was blaring so loudly that it could be heard above the traffic. It was 'Jingle Bells', Jill decided, turning round just in time to see the man with the brindle greyhound going through to the surgery. The boy with the box moved up a chair.

'I suppose you're next?' the woman asked him, and he told her he was, blowing out a sphere of bubble-gum, making her flinch. She began to complain, all over again, about having to wait. She kept on and on about it. She was that type, Jill decided, most probably spoiled by an adoring husband who granted her every whim. She was good-looking in a haughty way, was about Anna's age, or a little younger, but her face was spoiled by 'short-tempered' lines. 'My son is picking me up,' she said, looking straight at Jill. 'It's just as well he's not got here yet, for he *certainly* won't want to wait.'

For adoring husband substitute impatient son, Jill thought as the greyhound came out, and the boy with

the gerbil went in. Turning her face to the window, she
watched a young mother crossing the road with twins in
a buggy, hurrying to beat the lights. The day was bright,
but piercingly cold, and everyone was well wrapped up,
looking nipped and agonised, squinting against the sun.
In nine days' time it would be Christmas Eve and she,
Jill, would be on duty, singing carols in one of the many
choirs that toured the hospital.

A shape passed the window very close to, darkening it
for a second, then the street door opened, and Jill found
herself looking straight at Adam Greerson, who was
looking over at the tweed woman and crossing the floor
to her. Jill battled against the jumpy, shocked feeling
which always assailed her when she came across him
suddenly. It was like being thumped in the chest. His
back was towards her—he'd not seen her yet. He was
speaking to the woman, bending forward to her and
touching her on the arm. 'Don't fret so, Ma; I can wait
for you—I'm glad to get out of the crowds.'

Heavens above, so she was his mother! Jill digested
this, holding herself ready for the moment when he
would turn round and sit down. He did both these things
in one swift movement, unzipping his jacket, as he'd
done at Homewood last night, his hand stopping half
way down, as he caught sight of Barney and then her.
'Why, *hello* there!' He smiled, looking mildly discon-
certed, or perhaps he was just surprised.

'Good morning,' Jill answered, rather more formally.

'What brings you here?' He inclined towards her.
'Barney's not ill, I hope?'

'He needs his nails clipped, that's all.' She didn't
mention the dog's nether regions. She felt there was no
need to go into details, not with Mrs Greerson sitting
there bolt upright with the cat basket perched on her
knees.

Quickly Adam introduced her. 'This is Jill Arbor,

Mother. . .*Nurse* Arbor, whom I drove home last night. You remember I told you I met her grandmother. . .'

'The writer, Anna Stevens,' Elaine Greerson said promptly. She smiled too, quite pleasantly, as Jill got up and shook her hand. She even smiled at Barney, who was being held well out of reach. 'I've read *all* Anna Stevens's books,' she said. 'They give me so much pleasure.'

'I'm glad, and I'll tell her.' Jill straightened up.

'You're not like her, are you?'

'Not in looks or talent.' Jill returned to her chair.

'Except that to be a good nurse,' Mrs Greerson was bent on being magnanimous, 'must be a talent in itself.'

'More of a vocation, surely,' Adam put in drily, while his mother continued to size Jill up, her eyes moving over her much-washed blue jeans and thick baggy sweater. The girl looked incredibly young, far too young to be holding down a responsible senior nursing post.

'Where have you left Vanessa?' She turned to Adam again.

'In the post office, in the parcel queue.'

Jill pricked up her ears. Vanessa was probably the girlfriend Dick Lane had mentioned. Perhaps she was staying with the Greersons over the weekend. Adam's mother, she felt quite sure, would thoroughly approve of a girl who worked at the famous Rothenby's.

The inner door opened once more and the boy with the box came out. He went to the desk to pay the bill, and this time Clive Barnett—round-faced and smiling, his sandy hair slightly awry—appeared in the doorway, looking, Jill thought, like something out of James Herriot in his flapping veterinary coat. Dear Clive. . .it was good to see him. She half rose in greeting, then as he sighted her and waggled his fingers Mrs Greerson shot to her feet.

'*I'm* next!' she said in stentorian tones, ploughing

towards him and practically pushing him backwards into his room. The door closed, and Jill looked at Adam.

'I wasn't queue-jumping,' she said, 'but I know Clive Barnett—he wasn't calling me in.'

'I didn't think you were—don't worry about it.' He reached for a copy of *Horse and Hound*, which lay on a table near by. 'My mother is on edge about Seamus. He's an old cat now, and has started having epileptiform fits, which are very distressing to see.'

'Oh, of course—I'm sorry,' Jill said at once. 'What kind of cat is Seamus?'

'A white Persian, very handsome.' He put down the magazine and concentrated instead on Jill, thinking how different she looked out of uniform, although most women did, of course. Even in casual gear, however, she had an immaculate look; she was neatly boned, her skin was clear, and her bright hair glowed with health. 'Is Barney the last patient this morning?' His eyes moved to the dog, who, sensing that his time was near, had begun to judder his legs.

'I would think so, yes.' Jill looked at her watch. 'Clive doesn't usually work after eleven on Saturdays, although there's always a vet on call.'

Adam was about to comment on this when the street door opened and a girl in a black skirt and red leather jacket made her way over to him. 'Vanessa. . .so you made it!' He got up and sat her down on the chair beside his, relieving her of her bulging shopping-bag.

'I've finished, yes, but it's hell in the shops.' Her hair was long and black, loosely tied back with a ribbon and huge spectacles dwarfed her face.

'It's Christmas, in case you've forgotten.'

'I only wish I could!' Her mouth was large and brilliantly lipsticked, and when she smiled she showed beautiful teeth. The description 'exotic' fitted her exactly; she was like a hothouse bloom. Anna would rave about her, thought Jill just as Adam—for the second time in half an hour—launched forth into introductions. It was then she learned that the girl, or the woman, for she looked well into her thirties, was Vanessa Lawley. . .'Who, believe it or not, is a lady auctioneer!' Adam looked proud as this was explained.

Jill said, 'How interesting,' while Vanessa Lawley, who missed very little and had noticed the hole in Jill's sweater, said it could be the most tiring job on earth.

They began a three-way conversation that trickled, rather than flowed. It took quite a lot of keeping up, so perhaps they were all relieved when Mrs Greerson reappeared, followed by Clive carrying Seamus in his basket, and uttering reassurances about his condition. 'For an old cat, he's doing very well.' He spoke partly to Adam, who had got up to stand by his mother. Clive had met him once or twice before, here in the surgery. Jill hovered, ready to go in once the Greersons had paid their bill. Vanessa Lawley, clearly anxious to be off, stood a little apart from them all, tapping heel and toe on the vinyl floor, looking out into the street. In a matter of minutes they were filing out, Adam carrying Seamus. Jill said goodbye to them, standing by the desk alongside Clive, Barney wriggling on her hip.

'I didn't realise you knew the Greersons.' Clive gave Jill a hearty kiss in the privacy of the surgery, then bandaged Barney's muzzle, for when his nails were clipped he was apt to panic and bite.

'Adam Greerson is our new registrar; he started this week.'

'*Really*! I didn't know that.' Clive began to clip, soothing Barney and cutting carefully, so as to miss the quick. 'I knew he was a surgeon at a London hospital. . .his mum told me that.'

'He was at St Lukes, South Ken, but now he's with

us.' Jill tried to sound nonchalant, but overdid it. Clive gave her a searching look.

'Mrs Greerson has been living here for roughly a year,' he said. 'I've seen the girl about too—mostly at weekends.'

'She'd be difficult to miss.'

'You're telling me!' A grin spread over Clive's face. 'Pity she hasn't got a classy pet, wanting my expert attention.'

He was still the same old Clive, Jill thought. 'You get worse,' she laughed.

He shook his head. 'Not really, most of it's just talk. All right, old chap,' he stroked Barney's head, 'we won't be very long now.' The last nail was clipped, Barney's muzzle untied, his troublesome gland cleared. He was lifted down from the table, and Clive turned to scrub his hands. Jill watched his broad white back as he stood at the sink. He caught her eye in the mirror. 'So, how many hearts have you broken lately?' he asked her, without turning round.

'I don't let things get that far, Clive.' The soap he was using smelled of carbolic. He rinsed his hands and hung up his coat on the door.

'You're a nice girl, do you know that?' His greeny-grey eyes were bold.

'What a terrible description—it's almost an indictment!'

He shrugged. 'It's not meant to be.' She moved back to let him through and they stepped into the waiting-room. There was no one there. The chairs were bare and the receptionist had gone home. Clive set the answer phone to 'On', and reached for his jacket. He had two calls to make—one to a farm, the other to the home of an elderly lady who had a sick mynah bird.

'What are you doing this afternoon?' he asked her out in the street.

'Shopping mostly—Anna's working.'

He was feeling for his keys. He drew them, jingling, out of his pocket, clasped them tightly and said, 'You couldn't help me with mine, could you. . .Christmas shopping, I mean? I haven't done any yet, and I never know what to get.'

He'd have a lot to get, Jill knew that, for he had loads of relatives. He was the youngest in a family of six, most of whom lived in Northumberland. His brothers and sisters had all married and had offspring of their own, so present-buying, especially at Christmas, was quite a formidable task.

She thought about it, hesitated, then suddenly made up her mind. 'Yes, OK, Clive, you're on,' she said. He beamed and slapped her arm.

'Terrific! I'll pick you up at Windon around half-two, and when we've done we could have a cream tea at Dawsons, if you like.' He made for his car, which was parked in the sideway, and presently drove it out slowly past her, nudging carefully into the traffic stream.

CHAPTER FOUR

JILL was dismayed to learn from the report on Monday morning that during the weekend Mrs Emily Flood had suffered a stroke.

'She's being transferred to the medical floor some time before lunch,' Nurse Catling said, supplying more details after the night sister had left. 'It happened on Saturday morning. She was coming out of the bathroom, when she gave a sort of choking gurgle and collapsed in a heap on the floor. At first I thought she'd arrested, then I discovered a pulse. The medical registrar was sent for, and diagnosed a cerebral vascular accident. We were all very distressed.'

'Oh, dear, poor Mrs Flood!' Jill saw from the notes that Emily had lost the use of her left arm and leg, that her speech centre had been affected, and that her face and mouth had a droop.

'When she talks she sounds as though she's been at the sherry bottle.' Irene Catling edged her way to the door. 'What has amazed everyone is that little Miss Pink is so concerned about her—she really is a love. She spent over an hour yesterday, after her own visitors had gone, reading to her and talking to her, trying to get some response.'

'Patients never cease to surprise us, do they?' Jill got out Miss Pink's notes. Her discharge home had been confirmed for today; her sister was coming for her. This meant that Pharmacy would have to be asked to send up her take-away tablets. There was a new patient—one of Sir Rodney's—coming in for vagotomy. She would occupy Miss Pink's bed, and no doubt Emily Flood's had been earmarked for the next patient on the waiting list. Non-urgent admissions, as Jill knew, would be held up until after Christmas; they always were, and as many patients as possible were discharged. Picking up a pile of letters, which the postman had left on the desk, Jill entered the ward to distribute them—always a pleasant task.

Miss Pink had two letters—one a get-well card, the other from her nephew in Aberdeen. She settled down to read. Ruth Gardner was sitting out of bed, while Nurses Bell and Sibley straightened it, and plumped her pillows up. Ruth was still waxen pale, Jill observed, and her big blue eyes were heavily shadowed, but she had turned the corner: she was going to get well.

'I've been very ill, haven't I?' she said as Jill approached.

'Yes, you were, for a little while, but you put up a very good fight. A ruptured spleen means a massive blood loss, so we had to give you lots more. Still, you're making great strides now, and I'm sure the doctors will be pleased with you when they come round later on.'

Who would be coming? Jill wondered. Adam or Dick, probably both, and maybe even Sir Rodney as well. She tried to quell the nervous flutter that the thought of Adam invoked. She was getting on so much better with him, which had to be good news, but always remember Vanessa Lawley, and don't for one moment suppose that he sees you as other than a nurse, who has yet to prove herself, for he still doesn't quite rely on me, does he? He's still not sure that I'm up to the job—I can see the doubt in his eyes.

Out in the side-ward, Emily greeted her like a long-lost friend. She was very emotional, fat tears squeezing out of her eyes, while her unaffected 'good' right arm hooked itself round Jill's neck. 'Fell. . .shtroke. . .can't shpeak proper,' she managed to bring out in a bursting fashion, spit running out of her mouth.

'You'll improve, Emily. . .things will get better.' Jill took her hand. 'Once you get to the medical ward you'll have special care, and lots of physiotherapy to help you walk and talk again. Very often, as we think *you* will, patients who've had strokes make a complete recovery, so please remember that. Think positive, as Sister would say!' Jill was trying to get her to laugh.

'They told me. . .Livingshtone Ward.'

'Yes, that's where you're going, under the care of Dr Farne. He's very kind, and very clever; you'll be all right with him.' Jill managed to free herself from Emily's right hook, and stand upright again.

'But will I shee you before I go?'

'Of course; I'll take you down there, but they're not ready for you yet.' They probably, Jill thought, had a patient to discharge, and her bed to wash over and make up afresh, for the medical wards were as busy as surgical ones. 'You'll like it in Livingstone Ward; it's much quieter than up here,' she was saying as she left the side-ward, walking backwards into the corridor. And this was how she came to cannon straight into Adam, who was passing the doorway, and trample all over his feet.

'Oh, dear, I'm sorry!' She made the mistake of laughing as she apologised, partly out of nervousness. She flattened against the wall.

'Do you usually walk out of doorways backwards?' He looked as annoyed as his voice. His face was pained— perhaps his feet were still tender from the mountain bike incident.

'I'm very sorry,' she said again, and this time she looked contrite.

'All right, all right, let's get on!' He was obviously in a rush. Perhaps it wasn't quite the right time to tell him about Emily's stroke, but she felt she had to say something to dispel the atmosphere.

'It's not a severe stroke' she finished, 'but it really is a shame. . .such a pity; just as she was getting on so well.'

'Mrs Flood isn't my patient, Staff,' they were turning into the office, 'and no, that doesn't mean,' he added as he saw the look on Jill's face, 'that I don't give a damn about her, poor woman. What it means is that I have to confine my efforts to what and whom concerns me, which right now is Miss Gardner's condition, also Mrs Arnopp's, not to mention Mrs Timms's.'

With a feeling of having been firmly corrected, Jill turned to get out the notes. And it wasn't just what he had said so much as the way he had said it, and his out-of-temper demeanour, but, of course, she told herself, I don't know him all that well; he may be prone to moods. It wasn't just his bruised feet, she was sure; it had to be more than that. Perhaps his weekend had gone wrong; perhaps he'd quarrelled with his girlfriend. Well, whatever it was, he shouldn't bring it all the way up to the surgical floor and take it out on her.

'I'd like to look at Miss Gardner's wound,' he said as she faced him again, 'so lay up a trolley, will you, and bring it into the ward?' He took the three sets of notes from the top of the desk. 'I can manage without you, meantime.' He went off set-faced, snapping a brief good-morning to Rachael Marks, who was coming out of the sluice.

In Clean Utility Jill laid a dressing pack on top of the trolley, took scissors from a jar of spirit, found two disposable masks, forceps from a sterile drum, bandages and micropore, then wheeled it all into the ward and alongside Ruth Gardner's bed. Adam was already there, explaining to Ruth that he wanted to take a peep at her wound, and check the drainage tube. He had managed to soften his face in the process, and a good job too, Jill thought, handing him his mask.

The wound looked healthy, with no haematoma or signs of inflammation—just a neat curve of stitches running under Ruth's left ribs. The drainage tube was still oozing slightly, and it was to this that Adam paid the most attention, reassuring Ruth that on the whole she was doing remarkably well. 'By perhaps Wednesday or Thursday,' he said, 'we'll get you into the day-room— it'll give you a change of scene. I've got a patient in Charlestone Ward who's had a similar op to you. He's about your age, and he's fed up with having no one to talk to. . .other than the oldies, of course, which he calls the forty-year-olds!' He smiled at Ruth, who smiled back.

'Will I be all right up?' she said.

'By Wednesday, yes, you will, far more all right than sitting here, not being fully ambulant. We want your blood circulating healthily again, not forming itself into clots.'

'You'll be helped along there, Ruth; you won't have to go it alone,' Jill said, understanding the young girl's nervousness.

'OK, then, I'll do it,' she said, earning a smile from them both.

'That discharge,' Adam remarked to Jill, up at the ward desk, 'is pancreatic enzyme. Unfortunately the tail of her pancreas was injured as well. Still. . .' he rubbed his chin. . .'it should heal in a day or two. I'll write her up for oral probanthine, which should help things along; one t.d.s. before meals, two at bedtime.'

Mrs Timms, the strangulated hernia patient, he pronounced fit to go home. 'With my stitches still in, Doctor?' She gazed up at him with a mixture of delight and consternation on her thin, pixie face.

'You won't burst them,' he told her, 'not as long as

you take proper care. Your husband is retired, isn't he, and can keep an eye on you?'

'Oh, yes,' Mrs Timms nodded her head up and down like a mandarin, 'my Arthur can turn his hand to anything, even looking after me.'

'The community nurse,' Adam continued smoothly, 'will be calling on Wednesday or Thursday, to take out your stitches, but even then you'll have to take reasonable care, you know. Heavy lifting, or stretching up too high, is out for all time, not simply for the next few weeks.'

'I'll remember, Mr Greerson, thank you. I'm grateful for what you did.'

'It was a pleasure,' he assured her, and Mrs Timms was charmed.

But Jill wasn't liking him much at all, not in his present mood. He was fine with the patients, and polite to her, but only *just* polite. She had the feeling that he would like to find fault and tell her off for something, to vent his spleen, in other words, which, bearing in mind the work they were doing, was a pretty fair simile.

'As her stools are a normal colour now,' he said of Mrs Arnopp, 'arrange for a cholangiogram, if you will, then if the duct is normal the tube can be spigoted, and we'll see how she goes from there. If she gets no pain I'll remove the tube myself on Friday or Saturday.'

Jill wanted to tell him that she was quite capable of removing a T-tube, but wisdom prevailed and she held her tongue, as she followed him back to the office. There he bent over the desk to write out a script for Ruth Gardner; he scribbled in Mrs Timms's notes as well, and as Jill stood waiting she saw Joe out in the corridor, making signs to her. She knew he wanted to go into the ward, so nodded assent, turning to watch him walking between the two lines of beds, neat and trim in his dark trousers and white overall coat.

'If I could possibly have your attention, Staff. . .' Adam's voice made her jump. Turning from the viewing window, she met his impatient eye.

'Yes?' she asked, not looking away, and somewhere above their heads it seemed to her that swords clashed— she could hear the rasp of steel.

'I was about to say,' his eyes flickered slightly, 'that I think Mrs Irons would be a little more comfortable if I drained off some of that abdominal fluid. Anyway, I think it's worth doing.'

'You mean now?' she enquired.

'No, I don't.' He looked at his watch. 'Get her ready for eleven o'clock—I'll do it in the ward. Either you or Nurse Catling can assist me; I don't mind which.' He turned round as a heavy step sounded out in the corridor and a hand to match it pounded the office door. It was Mr Rule, the vascular surgeon, and as the two men hadn't met Jill introduced them, after which Adam went off. 'I'll be back in an hour,' he reminded Jill, who was glad to see him go.

Jonathan Rule wanted to examine Emily Flood. 'It's most unfortunate that she should have had this stroke,' he said testily, clicking with his tongue. It seemed that he, too, was in a tetchy mood. It must, Jill thought, be a pre-Christmas mood-bug peculiar to surgeons. She produced Emily's notes and then she and Jonathan Rule—a giant of a man with a massive jaw—went to the side-ward next door.

Emily was wearing firm crêpe bandages, and these Jill removed. Mr Rule examined her legs and groin, nodding in satisfaction. 'Tubigrip supports would be easier for her to manage at this stage,' he said as they left the ward. 'Pity about her stroke.'

'Fortunately it wasn't a very severe one,' Jill found bound to point out.

'And surgery in no way precipitated it; she was

mobilised early enough. I'll see her when she's been transferred to Livingstone. Dr Farne is an excellent man; she'll do well with him. Pity, though. . .great pity!' He went out, pulling his ear.

After laying up the trolley for Mrs Irons's paracentesis, Jill spent the next half-hour making transport arrangements for the patients who were being discharged that day. She also rang Haematology in an attempt to hurry up the reports on two specimens, and was just in the middle of a telephone argument with the laundry manager about some missing sheets, when Joe came to tell her that he had finished his treatments. As she was on the phone, she flapped a hand at him, and in doing so she knocked two folders on to the floor. Joe came in and picked them up.

'Thanks, Joe.' Her phone call ended, but she still felt rattled by it. 'That laundry manager wants soaping and rinsing in one of his machines,' she cried. 'I've never *heard* such language!'

'Oh, dear!' Joe looked sympathetic. 'It's one of those mornings, is it?'

'A morning and a half! We're one nurse short and Nurse Catling's not on till midday. All in all, you know, Joe, I shan't be sorry when Sister's back. I don't think I'm cut out for top-level management as yet.'

'Nonsense. Of course you are. You're doing a terrific job. You're not the sort to give up on anything, either, not without a fight.' Joe's hand came out and squeezed hers as it lay on top of the desk. He was only trying to reassure her, for he was that kind of man, but his hand was slow at withdrawing itself, and was only just moving off when Adam came in, wanting to do Mrs Irons's paracentesis.

'I take it you've finished in here, Buckman?'

His enquiring expression was only just slightly overdone, his tone of voice only just verging on the sardonic, so both were lost on Joe, who wasn't unduly sensitive. All he said was, 'Yes, thanks,' and went off.

Jill, however, felt acutely embarrassed, and betrayed this by flushing to the roots of her hair as she moved past Adam into the corridor. 'I've got Mrs Irons's trolley ready, if you want to do the paracentesis now,' she said.

'That's why I'm here!' He pushed at the left-hand ward door with the flat of his hand. 'Draw up two per cent lignocaine for the local, and I want to use a wide-bore cannula and trocar, so I'll need a scalpel as well.'

'I'll see to it.' Jill hurried off, still feeling embarrassed and, what was worse, she felt guilty too, which she knew was ridiculous. She hadn't been fooling around with Joe in any way at all, but of course it could have looked like that to an eye as jaundiced as Adam Greerson's was this morning. Damn and blast the man!

Mrs Irons was pleased at the prospect of getting rid of her ascites. 'Perhaps when it's all gone, Doctor, I'll be able to get about better.'

'You will, and you'll be able to breathe better too, and lie more comfortably,' Adam said, as Jill tied his gown and handed him his gloves. 'First of all I'm going to freeze the lower part of your tummy,' he told her. 'All you'll feel is a little prick, but I know you're used to injections.'

'Very used,' Mrs Irons said sadly as the needle went in. She lay quite still and looked at the ceiling while Adam and Jill carried out the small procedure, working together so smoothly and harmoniously that the two of them could have been one. Once the cannula was inserted and the trocar withdrawn, Adam slipped the rubber cuff firmly into position, while Jill made sure that the end of the long piece of tubing hung inside the bedside jar. The liquid began to drain freely and quickly.

'Couldn't be better.' Adam straightened up, ripping off his mask. Jill was attending to Mrs Irons, dressing the small entry wound and placing two hunks of absorbent wool on each side of her abdomen.

'In case of leaks,' she explained to her. 'You've been very good, Mrs Irons.'

'I second that,' Adam said, watching Jill replace the bedclothes and make her comfortable.

'All you've got to do is just lie there and drain off,' Jill explained, 'but, if you're worried about anything, press your bell. Now I'll draw your curtains back.' As she did so Adam slipped through them, and Nurse Bell came forward to remove the trolley; Jill joined Adam at the ward desk.

'Thanks for your help.' He was writing in the notes. Jill stared at his downbent head.

'I was glad to be able to help,' she said. 'I hadn't seen that type of paracentesis done for some time.'

'I'd never have known it.' He looked up and smiled, and she found herself smiling back. He appeared to have sloughed off his hedgehog mood, and as for me, I'm putty in his hands, she thought, loathing the cliché and deploring her lack of will where he was concerned. It was humiliating to be affected so strongly by another person's moods—a man's moods, moreover. It was so undignified.

'I think you said you were on duty over Christmas?' he remarked as they left the ward desk.

'I am, but I don't mind, though. I'm looking forward to it, especially the carol-singing on Christmas Eve in a *London* hospital. Somehow or other that gives me an extra thrill.'

'You're all for the traditional bit, are you?' They were passing the tree as he said this, and the look he gave it could have been wistful or withering. Jill couldn't decide which it was.

'I don't think there's anything wrong with tradition,'

she said, 'unless it's taken to silly lengths. Patients love to hear the carols, just as we love singing them.'

He made no comment at all on this, and once again Jill felt that she'd said too much, and ought to have held her tongue.

It was a busy week, that lead-up to Christmas, with so much to arrange. All over the hospital the various departments and wards were getting out duty rosters for skeleton staffs. Jill and Nurse Catling—knowing that some of the services would close down—stocked up on drugs, and dressings, and domestic supplies. As many patients as possible were being discharged home, but before they went they helped the nurses decorate the ward. Candles and paper-chains were taboo, due to strict safety limits; even so, the whole of the surgical floor looked a picture by Christmas Eve morning.

Several patients gave the nursing staff presents of chocolates and biscuits and fat bulbs in fancy pots brought in by relatives. Jill was touched to receive a bottle of sherry from Emily Flood, brought in by her stalwart husband, Bert. 'She can talk a lot better already, love.' Mr Flood called everyone love. 'She'll soon be home, bossing me about from pillar to post again; by New Year she'll be back with me.' Jill doubted this very much, but didn't say so. Emily Flood had a long way to go as yet.

Joe and Jill exchanged cards in the canteen at lunchtime. In the normal way, Joe didn't lunch as early as half-past twelve, but he had finished work at midday, and would soon be starting his long journey westward into Wales, to be with his family and his fiancée, Megan, who was already counting the hours.

Jill was off duty at teatime, so had four hours to kill before she was due to assemble in the hall with the Christmas carolling team. There were four separate choirs going round, taking different wings of the hospital. When they had all completed their 'musical tours' they were to meet in the boardroom, on the ground floor, for coffee and mince pies.

'There are ten males and twenty females in our lot,' Chrissie said, as they set about preparing a light meal before they went out. 'That's more than there were at rehearsal, but nearly every year there are a few late-comers, and the SNO doesn't mind—not when they've got a honey of a voice, as Adam Greerson has.'

'*Adam!*' Jill's fork clattered down; they were eating lasagne, the frozen kind, which was easy to prepare.

'I thought that would make you sit up.' Chrissie grinned, getting to her feet to shut the kitchen window— she was sitting in a draught. 'According to May Renfrew from the kids' ward, his voice is pure bliss. He's a baritone—she heard him being auditioned last night. She said he sang 'In the Bleak Mid-winter' from begin-ning to end. Apparently you could have heard a pin drop for minutes after he'd done. He'll probably be asked to sing solo tonight in one of the women's wards, and hold all the patients spellbound, right over to New Year's Day.'

'Shooting their temperatures up by degrees, if he's as good as all that,' Jill said, trying her hardest to sound reasonably unconcerned. He hadn't said anything about singing to her, but then, why should he? He might not have made up his mind until the last minute, anyway. 'Cupid is at work in the day-room,' she remarked presently, changing the subject, feeling uncomfortable under Chrissie's all-seeing eye.

'Between patients, you mean? Tell me more—where has his arrow landed?' Chrissie's interest was deflected, and Jill heaved a sigh of relief.

'Squarely in Ruth Gardner's heart,' she said. 'She and a boy from Charlestone, who's had a similar op, have been keeping close company since Wednesday. It seems

to be love at first sight. Ruth was terribly upset when
he—Don Chance—was discharged home today. She's
afraid he'll forget all about her, and of course he just
might. Hospital-patient romances are a little like holiday
ones—once ordinary life takes over, they eddy off like
dreams.'

'Well, if *we* don't start eddying off we'll never be
ready in time,' Chrissie said practically, stacking the
plates and taking them to the sink. After tidying up they
went to their respective rooms to get ready, changing
into clean uniforms, pinning on crisp bib aprons and
starched white caps with a sprig of holly clipped on to
the side.

Jill rubbed blusher into her cheeks, for she felt she
looked too pale. She was excited, and knew it—the
feeling surged inside her, tingled in her fingertips,
making her curl her toes, making her heart beat a little
faster, destroying her peace of mind. She knew, too,
what had brought this about—the news that Adam
would be with them tonight. . .this magic night. . .the
night that was Christmas Eve. Her eyes shone—she was
looking her best, and couldn't help knowing she did—as
she drew on her cloak, inside out to show the scarlet
lining, and fixed the straps, criss-crossed over her breast.

There was no sign of Adam, however, when she and
Chrissie crowded into the main hall just before nine p.m.
The male doctors, some thirty of them, were all in their
white coats, standing around talking and laughing with
the nurses, for during the festive season protocol flew
out of the window, at least until Christmas night.

'Gorgeous Greerson isn't in evidence,' Chrissie whispered in Jill's ear as they were divided up into suitable
groups. Their group was being presided over by Miss
Seyton, the nursing officer, second in command to the
SNO.

'Perhaps he's thought better of it,' Jill said, just as the

doors revolved once more to admit the very man they were talking about.

'You're late, Mr Greerson; we were just about to move off without you,' Miss Seyton said, handing him a lantern on a pole.

'I'm glad I was able to make it.' Adam's tone was agreeable. Yet he's still managed to make the point that we're lucky to have him, Jill thought, turning to say hello to him.

The geriatric wards were the first to be visited, and the carollers were grouped plumb in the middle, where the doors that divided male patients from female had been drawn back against the walls. A neat semicircle was formed, the doctors at the back, holding the lanterns, the nurses in front. Adam was right behind Jill.

They sang 'The First Noel', Miss Seyton conducting, her bolster figure tightly encased in her navy dress, arms dipping and swaying. Jill, who'd had voice training during her last year at school, came into her own when she sang. It was like a kind of release to open her mouth and hear the sound pouring out of her throat. And to sing in hospital, to sing at Christmas, to sing to patients, in chorus with friends and colleagues, was a healing, wonderful thing.

She was aware of Adam singing behind her, was aware that his voice and hers made a combination of sound that lifted the choir into the realms of near star-quality, instead of just merely good. 'Hark! the herald angels sing' was rendered in Orthopaedics, but once they made for the children's ward Miss Seyton announced that she would like Mr Greerson and Nurse Arbor to sing the next carol in duet. Everyone was in agreement with this. Jill was taken aback. 'Whatever is she thinking about?' she whispered to Adam as they all started the long walk to the paediatric wing.

'She's thinking that we both have good singing voices,

and, of course, she's right,' he said, smiling broadly; he was plainly enjoying himself. Didn't anything ever unseat him, Jill wondered, or diminish his confidence? 'It'll be perfectly all right, you know.' He gave his lantern a hitch. 'We're unlikely to be slow-handclapped, or have anything thrown at us, not on Christmas Eve.' He fell into line at the back again, and Chrissie gave Jill a nudge.

'He fancies you rotten,' she said *sotto voce*. 'Half the nursing staff would like to be in your shoes tonight.'

'I'm singing with him, not sleeping with him!' Jill was quick to retort, but Chrissie only giggled and reminded her—nudging her again—that all good things came to those who waited.

Entering the children's wing was like a walk into fairyland. Every cot and bed had been decorated differently, every windowpane had a stencil, every child had a stocking, as yet unfilled, for Santa Claus was bashful and wouldn't appear till the singers had gone and everyone was asleep. At one end of the main ward, set up on a table for safety, was a Nativity scene with a painted night sky, showing the star in the east.

Some of the toddlers were already asleep, but most of the older children were awake and watchful, except those who were very ill. At the sight of them all—and sick children always tugged at the heartstrings—Jill forgot her nervousness, as she and Adam began to sing the age-old carol that all small children loved:

'O little town of Bethlehem,
How still we see thee lie!
Above thy deep and dreamless sleep
The silent stars go by. . .'

'Thank you so much, that was lovely!' the sister on duty enthused. One or two children echoed her words, and one little boy, flat on his back in a plaster bed, raised his arms and clapped his hands.

'Away in a Manger' came next, with the whole choir singing. They moved to the Nativity scene for this, which gave them a view of the two wards, of all the children, even the babies and toddlers—some standing up in their cots, some peeping through the bars. There were mothers with several of them. Some would stay all night in the parents' room, like a dormitory, just outside the ward doors.

The evening wore on, more wards were visited, more carols were sung. The last but one call was to Livingstone Ward, and as they filed in Jill waved to Emily Flood, who waved her 'good' arm back. Here they sang 'Good King Wenceslas' before going upstairs to Ecclestone Ward, where, after the singing was done, Mrs Flixton called for three hearty cheers for the Walbrook Choir.

'Just a little muted clapping, no cheers,' Miss Seyton stipulated. 'It may be Christmas Eve, but this is still a hospital ward.'

It was nearly eleven o'clock when the four choirs met up and made their way to the old boardroom, where hot mince pies and coffee were wheeled in by the SNO herself. 'Another half-hour and my throat would have burst,' Dr Charles Farne declared. He, Adam, Jill and Chrissie were all sitting together. Others joined them; everyone was happy; the spirit of Christmas could be felt like a presence in that hot overcrowded room.

Charles Farne soon made movements to go. 'I'm taking my wife to midnight Mass,' he explained, then turned in an aside to Adam. 'You must come and have a meal with Anne and me some time—bring a friend, if you like.'

'Thanks very much.' Adam got up and walked to the door with him. They stood and chatted for a few minutes, and, watching them standing there, Jill tried to analyse her feelings. What did she *really* feel about Adam, other than attraction of the physical kind? He interested her, she was curious about him, she wanted to know more about him. He was ambitious, she knew that, but he was dedicated too. He also minded about people, and by that she meant the patients. She had begun to like him, she realised that, but something was warning her to stop that liking right where it was. . .not to let it deepen, or ripen into anything else, for she'd simply be wasting her time. He's right out of my world, she told herself firmly, then laughed gaily at a joke that Dick was telling and helped herself to another hot mince pie. She was finishing it when Adam came back and took the chair beside her.

'I'm feeling the strain—I don't know about you.' He let his breath out in a puff.

'A little, perhaps.' She wiped her fingers on a paper serviette, staring down at its holly design. 'But it's been a good evening.'

'Absolutely—I enjoyed it.' She heard him clear his throat. People were talking and laughing all round them, sheltering them like a wall.

'And I'm luckier than you,' she told him, I haven't got to journey home.' She knew he was driving home and wouldn't be back until Boxing Day.

'I shall have to get started in a minute.' He almost had to shout against the gales of laughter coming from the centre of the room, where someone had hung a mistletoe bough, with the usual result. 'We're missing all the fun, Jill.' His arm moved along the back of her chair, and she felt herself tense, felt his breath warm on her cheek. His free hand turned her head, turned her face to his. . .she saw it in close-up for a fleeting second before he closed the space between them and brought his mouth to hers. A tide of sweetness swept through her. . .she hadn't expected to feel like that. . .not quite like that. . .like flying, like soaring, like wanting him madly. She found herself kissing him back.

It was quickly over, and all she was left with was his hand holding hers. He was smiling at her; the room looked the same; nothing seemed to have changed. There were the same gales of laughter coming from under the mistletoe. She tried to say something amusing and flip, but he beat her to it. 'There are some things about the festive season that raise my spirits, Jill. Perhaps. . .' he glanced away from her over to the kissing crowd '. . .perhaps I should go and try my luck with the SNO herself.'

'It would make her day—or, rather, night!' Jill straightened her cap. She was glad she was able to hide her feelings, to treat the whole thing as a joke. 'I think we should *both* circulate,' she added, 'and distribute our favours all round.'

She didn't catch Adam's reply, for as she got up to go she was immediately seized by Jonathan Rule, who told her how pretty she looked. Being hugged by him was like being crushed between sterile clamps. She had to be receptive, and bear it, but once she was released. . .and breathing again. . .it was to find that Adam had gone.

CHAPTER FIVE

THE ward routine was completed at top speed on Christmas morning, partly because there were fewer patients, but also because there were no interruptions in the shape of porters, social workers, and the like. Nurses Bell and Sibley were on duty, Irene Catling was off, but a nurse from Geriatrics had been 'borrowed' to make the numbers up. By ten a.m. beds and baths were done, drugs and dressings out of the way, and the patients happily settled with mid-morning drinks.

'The carol-singing was brilliant, wasn't it?' Dick enthused to Jill in the ward kitchen, where he was drinking coffee and dipping into the tin of biscuits left by Miss Pink for the nursing staff.

'Yes, it was, I enjoyed it,' Jill said guardedly, bringing to mind the way she had felt when she'd sung in duet with Adam and, later, the way she had gloried in his kiss. The memory of that swift embrace had stayed with her all night, agitating her dreams when she had slept, filling her thoughts when awake.

Dick kissed both her and the geriatric nurse before he left the ward. 'It's Christmas, girls, so I have to take my pleasures when I can!' He had probably taken them in Charlestone Ward, *and* eaten their goodies as well, Jill thought, closing the biscuit tin.

Most of the patients were able to enjoy the turkey and plum pudding lunch that came down from the main kitchens just after twelve midday. The nurses had theirs afterwards, taking it in turns to go up to the staff canteen; they returned full of praise for the catering staff, who had done a mammoth job. As Miss Cooper, the SNO, said when she visited the ward, the days were gone when the senior consultants carved a turkey on the ward, and sat down with the staff to eat it there. 'They value their off-duty more now,' she said, 'they put their families first, and who can blame them, considering the hours they put in during ordinary times?' Jill didn't blame them in the very least, and I doubt very much, she thought, if the nurses really enjoyed themselves, eating in such august company. It was best to 'keep to one's own lot', even on Christmas Day.

When the visitors filed in during the afternoon, many bringing gifts, tea was served to them, along with the patients, and no one bothered to ring the bell for the end of visiting; many rules were relaxed.

Boxing Day, however, was different—the other side of the coin. It began much the same, almost as much *en fête* as Christmas Day, but during the late afternoon, just as dusk was setting in, Miss Seyton arrived on Ecclestone Ward, grave-faced and important, with the news that the Walbrook had been put on major alert. 'There's been an accident on the motorway, over twenty vehicles involved, two of them coaches; we're to share the casualties with St Mildred's and St George's. Casualty are operating their disaster plan, and are awaiting the first ambulances now; Ecclestone and Charlestone are on standby, as the main receiving wards. No member of staff is to go off duty till we know the extent of it all. Put up extra beds, if you have to; the side-wards will each take two, and you've got,' Miss Seyton ran her finger down the bed list, 'five empty ones in the main ward. All right, then, Staff,' she was slightly breathless, 'over to you, but first get rid of the visitors—it's time they went anyway,' and she glared at the little family groups through the viewing window, as though she would have liked to sweep them out with a broom.

In the clinical-room, collecting together bed-cradles,

drip-stands, ventimasks and bowls, Jill's thoughts went
to the scene of the accident; she could see in her mind's
eye the glittering road, the wrecked cars, the rescue
vehicles; she could see the team of doctors and nurses
sent out from the hospitals, giving pain relief for victims
still trapped, setting up drips, making spot-on assess-
ments as to which casualties should be taken off first.
She could see the lights, hear the firemen, the grind of
their cutting instruments, see the police diverting the
traffic, the first ambulances moving off. 'It may be some
time,' she said to Nurse Marks, 'before we get busy up
here. The urgent cases will go straight to Theatre, but
I'll go down to Cas in half an hour's time, and find out
what the situation is.'

'It's probably chaotic.' Rachael and Jill were making
bed-packs in the side-wards. 'They'll call in all the
medical help they possibly can.' Rachael Marks had seen
it all before; she didn't really need to be primed and
prompted by Jill—not that she minded; the two young
women liked one another and worked together well.

The mêlée in Casualty, when Jill went down there,
made her halt in her tracks. Every cubicle was occupied,
and there were patients on trolleys in the corridors and
aisles. Ambulances were still bringing the injured in; the
waiting area was chock-a-block with walking wounded;
bewildered children were clinging to parents or junior
nurses; patients in wheelchairs looked dazed and sick
with shock.

The staff were coping magnificently. Many off-duty
nurses had come over from the nurses' home when they
had heard about the alert. On-call surgeons and doctors
were there in full spate—Adam being one of them, and
even then, in the midst of all that chaos and horror, Jill's
heart lifted. He was standing near the entrance doors
with Casualty Sister; they were taking details from the
ambulancemen, whose information was vital in assessing

the seriousness of each case they brought in. The victims were being sorted into 'critical', 'urgent' and 'non-urgent', then wheeled to the cubicles for treatment. Some were rushed straight to Theatre. Other patients were still coming in; the phones rang continuously; a child screamed; a girl had hysterics on learning that her boyfriend was dead; a baby was brought in with breathing difficulties. The smell of blood, and vomit, and petrol hung heavy on the air. Jill caught a glimpse of Charles Farne trying to hold an oxygen mask over the nose and mouth of a man who was fighting to push it away. At last she managed to reach the doors to ask Sister and Adam if they could tell her how soon Ecclestone Ward might be getting its quota of patients.

'We're sending two up any minute, to be prepped for surgery; there are three in Theatres, two of them critical. . . All right, you're safe now, old chap.' Adam was bending down to a small boy of six or seven, lying supine on a stretcher, crying in terror at the sight of his legs, which the ambulance men had splinted together. His nose was bleeding and the blood was running into his mouth.

Feeling in the way, a mere onlooker, Jill returned to the ward. She was urgently needed there, she knew, but if only, if only she could split herself in two and help down in Casualty as well. And why, she thought, do these shocking things happen? Why aren't drivers more careful on the motorways when winter conditions make things so hazardous? She had learned that today's accident had been caused by the speeding driver of a Jaguar car, who had hit the back of a minibus full of children. The bus had swerved over the hard shoulder, hit an oncoming van, and another car had hit the van, so the pile-up action had been repeated on both sides of the motorway. It didn't bear thinking about.

As things turned out, the emergency ward took most

of the accident cases. Ecclestone Ward had six of them, and all were able to be accommodated in the side-wards, which was a great relief to Jill, who had been dreading having to cancel the listed admissions booked in for next day. The five beds in the main ward were still available, so no one would have to be put off, or turned away, which occasionally happened when emergencies arose.

Three of the accident victims simply had cuts and bruises; another had a badly lacerated thigh, which had been sutured in Theatre; another had visceral injuries, while one elderly lady had two fractured ribs and a punctured lung, which meant that she had to be put on underwater seal drainage to get rid of all the 'free' blood.

Jill remained on duty till the night staff arrived at nine p.m., when there was extra briefing to be done, via the hand-over report. She had just finished and was leaving the office, when she saw a tall, raincoated figure backing out of the second side-ward. It was Adam, she saw to her relief as he turned and faced her. 'Heavens,' she gasped, 'I thought you were a prowler. . .how you startled me!'

'Sorry.' He passed a hand over his head, and she saw how weary he looked. All his lines were emphasised, and a sweep of feeling that had something of the maternal in it made her long to take charge of him. I wish he were mine, was the thought in her head, while her voice, which sounded as weary as his, had an accusing note.

'I didn't realise you were on the ward.'

'You were busy in there,' he nodded towards the office, 'and I didn't need a chaperon. I've just done a round of the accident cases.'

'They've all settled down. I'd have bleeped you if I was worried, or got Dick Lane.'

'But I also,' he went on doggedly, 'wanted to see if you'd gone off duty. You look about as bushed as I feel.' A gentle hand closed over her shoulder and eased her away from the wall. 'What we both need is a good stiff drink, and, as we've finished for the day, and as we're neither of us driving, I suggest that's what we have.'

The junior night nurse was taking a bedpan into the ward, and the senior yelled at her to put a cloth over it. It was hardly the place for a tryst, thought Jill, biting down on laughter, which might have verged on the hysterical. 'You mean, have a drink together?' she asked Adam, blinking up at him.

'There's no law against it.' He smiled at her, and some of his lines disappeared.

'No, of course not. I think it's a good idea.' She tried to hide her surprise. And why *be* surprised? It was Boxing night, and they'd both been through the mill. She'd been asked out for a drink before, by other doctors, on several occasions. There was really no need to be so overwhelmed because Adam had done the same thing. He was walking away now, and she realised that he'd not expected her to refuse.

'I'll meet you downstairs in five minutes,' he said, 'by the indicator board.'

In the cloakroom Jill rubbed compressed powder over her nose and cheeks, unpinned her cap, combed out her hair, took her heavy velour coat out of the locker, and buttoned it up to her chin. Her hair gleamed gold against it; her pale face was framed in its collar. I'll pass, she thought, feeling a thrill of unbridled excitement shoot through her, putting paid to her fatigue. I'm glad you thought of this,' she said, a few minutes later, as Adam steered her across Charterhouse Street to the Goldsmith Arms.

'I abound with good ideas,' he replied, pulling her back as a motorbike zoomed past them, practically on their toes. 'Relaxation is essential if one is to keep sane. You've been on duty since breakfast, while I've seen enough human misery in the past five hours to make me want to crawl into a hole in the ground. The parents of that small boy, the one with the fractured femur, both died—the father in the ambulance, the mother in Theatre, while I did my level best to take shards of metal out of her chest. She was four months pregnant; she didn't stand a chance.'

'Oh, Adam!' She used his Christian name without thinking twice about it. 'But you and Dick and Sir Rodney worked miracles; everyone said you did.'

Adam made no comment on this, and she wondered if he thought she was being overly fulsome, piling it on a bit thick. As it happened, she meant every word she said, and perhaps he did believe her, for, in spite of everything, she could see him starting to relax as they sat at their table in the lounge of the ancient inn that had once been a coaching house.

She was drinking a glass of white wine, he Scotch on the rocks. 'How did Christmas Day go?' he asked conversationally.

'Yesterday? Oh, terrific!' She smiled and told him about it. He sat and listened, not interrupting, and it struck her, not for the first time, that he had a way of keeping quiet while other people talked. To be a good listener was essential in a doctor. He would have made a good GP, except, of course, that his skill in the theatre, which Dick had told her about, would never have seen the light of day. Dick even said that he rivalled Sir Rodney in some of his techniques. 'I heard,' she said as she finished recounting the events of Christmas Day, 'that Miss Pink visited Mrs Flood down on Livingstone Ward.'

'That was good of her.' Adam set down his glass on the little round mat provided for that purpose, and looked at her. 'She can't be feeling all that chirpy herself yet,' he added.

'No, she can't.'

'I shall be seeing her in clinic in two weeks' time. I like Miss Pink; she has grit and courage and, under all that, a very kind heart. Anyway,' he sat back a little, 'how is Mrs Flood. . .even though she's not my patient?' and now he was teasing, making Jill feel a shade uncomfortable, remembering her brush with him.

'She's improving markedly.' She met his eyes square on. 'She can talk much more plainly, she can walk with help, and, as she was originally a surgical patient, Joe is treating her.'

'Then she'll improve, won't she, by leaps and bounds?' Adam said, and this time Jill wasn't quite so sure about the look in his eye.

'Joe Buckman is a good physio,' she felt compelled to say.

'And one of your string of admirers?'

'Well, that's what comes of being so peerlessly beautiful,' she said with a dead-pan face, and he laughed out loud, as she'd intended, and the awkward moment passed.

The Goldsmith Arms was popular with medical staff from the Walbrook. It was close at hand, it served snack meals, and its atmosphere was such that one forgot things like illness and dying as soon as one opened its doors. Sometimes shop was talked, of course, but even the most serious kind took on a more hopeful slant when two streets away from its source.

As Adam looked about him he couldn't help but notice the interested male glances directed at Jill, which didn't surprise him, not in the very least. She might not be 'peerlessly beautiful', but attractive she certainly was, with her pale gold hair, her long-lashed eyes, and slender, curving figure. She had thrown her coat over the back of her chair, and he could see the thrust of her breasts against the thick cotton of her belted uniform dress. He knew so little about her, and he wanted to know more, so decided to probe, just a little, without involving himself too far.

'So, what will you be doing for New Year? I think you said you were off duty.' And this was a fair enough question to start the ball rolling, he felt.

'I'll be going home,' she answered readily.

'To Windon?'

'That's my home.' There was a second's silence while she took a sip of wine, then said, 'Homewood has always been my home—I was brought up there. My parents were killed in the Wharton train disaster, four years ago. Dad worked in London—he used to commute. He was on that train, and so was my mother on that particular morning; she was going up to Christmas shop.'

'My God, how terrible!' Their eyes met and she saw the compassion in his. 'I remember the accident, remember it well.' He paused for a moment, then said, 'Three London hospitals shared the casualties. St Luke's, though, being out at South Ken, wasn't one of them.'

'My parents were killed instantly—they never got to hospital. They were in the first coach, and they died together. That's. . .what they would have wanted.'

'Where were you then?' His eyes were still kind.

'At the Bexford General, she said, 'in my second year. I lived in afterwards—at the hospital, I mean. Homewood was left to me. I let it for a time—I was advised to do so. I didn't want to sell it, anyway. I used to go down to Cornwall, to Anna, for holidays. We'd always been close, and when she told me she wanted to move nearer to London we talked it over, and she bought Homewood, after my tenants had left.'

'What a good idea.'

'It was the best for both of us. We were both alone, you see. My grandfather, who was much older than Anna, had died the year before, and, apart from her roots, which she says "pooh" to, there was nothing to keep her in Fowey. She's grown to love Hertfordshire, says that it's given her a new lease of life.'

'She looks young for her age.'

'She's sixty-six, but don't tell her I told you that!'

'Hand on heart.' He tapped his chest and both of them laughed.

After he had replenished their drinks he told her about his parents. 'They divorced when I was fifteen—we were living at Oxford then. Father was. . .still is. . .an orthopaedic consultant. Anyway, he married his registrar— certainly not for her looks!—but they suit one another; I go to see them as and when I can. They're still at Oxford, still working, both of them in their sixties. My mother decided to move this way just under a year ago. She has a cousin out at Hemel Hempstead, recently back from abroad. The two gravitate together occasionally, although Mother has speedily integrated into what I would term the "Bexford society". She's socially inclined, and I'm glad of that. No one likes seeing a parent unhappy, do they? And Ma was, for a very long time.'

'Yes, well, divorce is terrible.'

'An unhappy marriage is worse. I don't speak from experience, I hasten to add, but just occasionally an onlooker sees most of the game, which is not one I mean to play.'

'You're against marriage?' They were getting in deep. It's the drink, Jill thought, it's loosening our tongues. Perhaps we should stop before we get to the point of divulging things that might make us embarrassed later on.

'I'm not against it for other people, only for myself. It's not a state that appeals to me, not a commitment I wish to make. My work is my commitment,' he finished, and before Jill could comment he asked her what her aims were, what she wanted out of life. Looking at him, she decided to be truthful, for it seemed that kind of night.

'I'd like to get married one day,' she said, 'have a family, all that kind of thing, but I'm in no hurry. At the moment I, too, am committed to my work.'

'So you've not met the man of your dreams yet?'

She looked at him more sharply. Was he being sarcastic again? She decided he probably was. 'Not yet, no,' she told him coolly.

'But you're looking?'

'All the time.'

This made him laugh, and once again things were easy between them. Being with him is like riding on a roller-coaster, she thought, finishing her drink, and telling him that she thought she ought to go. 'If I don't I'll be fit for nothing tomorrow.'

He nodded and agreed. 'The same goes for me. It's been enjoyable, Jill.'

'Yes, it has.'

He rose when she did, and helped her on with her coat. His fingers brushed her neck as he did so, and her flesh leapt to his. Swiftly, with bent head and shaking hands, she buttoned up her coat, tying the belt with a swift savagery, nearly cutting off her breath.

The public bar was crowded as they passed through it on their way to the doors. Across the road in the King's Head a disco was in full swing, the throb of music vying with the snarl of traffic fighting its way down Farringdon Street for a night out in the West End. It was Boxing night, the night for revelry. All over London, from Aldgate to Kensington, from Chelsea to Hampstead, and all points beyond, there would be parties and panto-mimes, dances and discos, festive get-togethers in private houses to play charades and games.

'Well, there's one thing about living in—it's convenient,' Adam remarked as they crossed Charterhouse Street again and entered the hospital precinct. The doctors' residence and the nurses' home, not far from the medical school, lay to the east of Beyton Wing, just beyond Casualty. To get there they had to cross a wide yard, then a narrow street which divided the new building from the old. Once in the ancient courtyard with its fountains and seats, its cobblestones and brick paths, the lighting was more dim, glowing rather than gleaming from the globes of old-fashioned lamps.

'This is the part I like most of all, it's so wondrously old.' Jill wanted Adam to feel the same, and apparently he did.

'Yes, it's like being caught in a time warp, isn't it?' His hand came under her elbow. 'Ignore the pelt of the traffic outside—substitute horses' hoofs, and we could be back in Charles Dickens's time, more than a hundred years ago.'

'The lamps give that illusion.' Jill halted and lifted her face. 'When you look at them you expect to see a flame instead of a bulb.'

'Yes,' he said softly, and he stood back and watched her, as though seeing her for the first time, seeing her with the lamplight spilling over her like a shawl, making luminous pools of her eyes, shrouding her muffled figure in mysterious outline, her shadow, behind her, immobile on the stones. He stepped towards her, took her arm again, and as they moved on, beyond the lamps and into the darkness, their two shadows slipped past them, like the sinewy ghosts of a man and a girl who had walked there long, long ago.

Jill shivered, and he drew her closer. 'Come on, you're getting cold.'

'It's a goose walking over my grave,' she laughed. 'I'm not really cold.'

'All the same, best foot forward.' He urged her along,

out of the courtyard, down the path alongside the chapel, to the easterly yard and car park, and over to Cade House.

In the lee of the giant Christmas tree to the side of the steps, they turned to one another. 'Thank you for asking me out—I enjoyed it,' Jill said shyly, looking up at him.

'So did I.' His voice was soft, very nearly caressing. She knew he was going to kiss her, knew she wanted him to. Her heart pounded, thundered in her ears. She could see him standing there, patched in colours cast by the Christmas tree lights. A lantern from a needled branch glowed behind his head. The night was damp, and she could smell the pine. He and the tree seemed indissoluble, perhaps both moved—she really couldn't tell. All she knew was that his hands were touching her at last, were moving upwards to stroke her face, were sifting through her hair. 'Like silk, floss silk, like golden rain.' His gently murmured words were a puff of sound against her cheek, then his arms closed round her, hard, protective, drawing her in to him. When she moved her face and saw his mouth less than an inch from her own, when their lips met, moved, clung, when the kiss took fire, she gave herself up to it, soaring, flying, oblivious to everything but his dear self, his dear body like whipcord against her own.

And when it finished, when it was over, when they drew apart at last, he didn't try to be clever, or tease, or make a flippant remark. All he said was, 'Goodnight, my dear,' and watched her go up the steps. When she raised her hand at the top, just before the doors slid apart to receive her, he called out, 'Sleep well,' then moved off into the dark.

As for Jill, she reached her room and sat down in a state of entrancement. His kiss had shaken her to the core. She could still feel it on her lips, still feel the steely wrap of his arms, hear the murmur of his voice.

For him it had been an interlude, a fitting end to the evening. She knew that—she wasn't a fool, she didn't delude herself. Vanessa Lawley was his mistress. Deliberately she used the old-fashioned word, pushing it around like a pebble in her mind. I must never, she thought, lose sight of that fact. I must never allow myself to be alone with him again while off duty, for I could very easily get to the brink—that so dangerous brink—of falling in love with him.

CHAPTER SIX

JILL was on lates next day, and when she got to the ward it was to learn from Nurse Catling that the listed admissions had all been settled in. 'Dick came up to make a routine check. He and Mr Greerson are in the second side-ward at the moment with the chest accident case. Rachael is escorting them,' Irene Catling explained.

'Oh, fine.' Jill took the notes from her and started to read them up. She hadn't got far before she heard Adam and Dick coming out of the side-ward. A second later they were in the office, and, a little dry in the mouth, but otherwise calm, she was treating them both to the same 'good morning', relieved to see that, although he smiled, Adam appeared to be entirely patient-occupied, which was as it should have been, of course.

Three of yesterday's accident cases were able to be discharged. Jill went off to deal with these, and to make their travel arrangements. Soon after that the luncheon trolleys came down from the kitchens. Adam and Dick went off in a hurry. Jill saw them making for Charlestone Ward, via the day-room, while she was trying to persuade Miss Gulliver, one of the new patients, to eat some shepherd's pie.

She dealt with the hand-over report during the quiet hour, then went into the ward to help Ruth Gardner dress, and clear out her locker. Ruth was going home, to her parents in Seftonbridge; her father was coming for her. She was low in spirit, and very, very subdued. 'You see, I'd rather,' she told Jill, blowing her nose, 'be going back to the Highgate flat.' Ruth shared the top of a

96

house with two other girls, all of them secretaries in a big advertising firm.

'Your parents will spoil you, cosset you a little, which you can do with at the moment,' Jill said, folding her dressing-gown and laying her slippers on top.

'I dread the journey—two hours in the car. Daddy's a careful driver, but I'm still scared. . .I'm scared rigid.' Tears welled up in Ruth's eyes.

'Look, Ruth,' Jill sat on the bed, 'when you had your accident you were sitting in the back of a furniture van, and when it braked you were thrown forward on to a bar, which caused your injury. Now, that's a one-off, isn't it? It's not going to happen again. Today you'll be sitting in your father's car, with your seatbelt in position. You've said yourself that he's a careful driver—*you'll be all right*. It's a perfect day for motoring too. . .' a glance at the window showed sunshine instead of fog '. . .and you'll be home well before dark.'

'I'm a shocking coward.' Ruth managed a smile.

'That's the last thing you are. You've been very brave all through,' Jill assured her, just as a hand swept the curtains aside, to show Adam looking in.

'You've been a model patient, Ruth. I can vouch for that,' he said.

'I bet you say that to all the girls!' Ruth was cheering up.

'Only to those who deserve it.' He moved back to let her stand up. 'Now remember to come back for your OPD appointment in four weeks' time.'

'I've got my card.' Ruth plunged a hand into her pocket to make sure, her limp brown hair, which she was dying to wash, parting at the back. She wasn't standing perfectly upright—her young thin shoulders were bowed. She had been very ill, and still wasn't strong. Jill felt protective towards her, and perhaps Adam did too. She was looking at him and holding out

her hand. 'Well, goodbye and thank you, Mr Greerson.
I'll never forget what you did.'

He took her hand and shook it. 'It was a team effort,
Ruth,' and he glanced at Jill, purposely including her.

'Oh, yes, of course, I *know*. Everyone's been good, so
good to me, but you two especially. I'm so grateful. . .'
But at that point Ruth stopped, her face pink; she was
looking over Jill's shoulder towards the doors. 'There's
Don—Donald Chance—he said he'd try to get here to
see me. You'll let him come in. . .let him stay, won't
you? I know it's not visiting time but. . .'

'It's not far off.' Turning round, Jill saw the lanky
form of Donald Chance, saw his bearded face looking
down into Nurse Bell's. She was shaking her head, so
she was probably stopping him coming into the ward.
Jill went off to deal with the matter, Adam following,
with the result that a few minutes later Ruth and her
new boyfriend were ensconced in the day-room, chairs
pulled together, heads even closer still, talking nineteen
to the dozen, fingers intertwined.

'Love's young dream,' Adam muttered.

'Well, don't knock it,' Jill smiled.

'I'm not—I'm envious,' he said quietly, surprising her
so much that she halted right there in the middle of the
ward, till he urged her forward, saying that he wanted to
see three more patients, including Mrs Leaming. 'She
was dozing when I came up earlier, and I hadn't the
heart to wake her. The poor woman needs all the rest
she can get.'

Nora Leaming was the most serious of the remaining
accident cases. Due to lung injury, causing free blood to
seep into her pleural cavity, she was on underwater seal
drainage; she was also being tranfused. Lying,
exhausted, back on her pillows, she was awake when
they went in. She looked with faint alarm at Adam, then
her gaze slewed to Jill. She was a bird-like little woman,

with small dark eyes, and a curved nose that nearly hid her thin parted lips. 'Hurts to breathe.' She was very dyspnoeaic.

Adam nodded sympathetically. 'Yes, I'm afraid that will continue for a while, but ease as each day passes.' His eyes were on the length of tubing running from her chest into the jar of water on the floor. There was blood in the jar, making spirals in the water, and there was whole new blood in the bottle suspended from the giving-set above Mrs Leaming's head. This was being run into her arm to replace what she had lost. Her eyes moved upwards to it, then down to the jar on the floor.

'Pity. . .that lot. . .can't be put back in.' She managed a faint smile.

'Recycled, you mean?' Adam was appreciating the joke. 'Medical science hasn't progressed that far yet, Mrs Leaming. All this equipment looks alarming, doesn't it? But it's doing its job, and *you* are doing wonderfully well. You're my best patient so far.'

Mrs Leaming's eyes gleamed amusement between half-closed lids. She wasn't taken in by Adam's blarney, ill though she was.

'Discontinue the transfusion once she's through that bottle,' he instructed Jill in the corridor, 'after which I think Sir Rodney will want to see her, probably this evening. Meantime, restrict her visitors to one—to her husband, if he comes. I don't want her making any sort of effort—the poor woman needs to rest. What about the thigh patient?'

'She's in side-ward three, and she's a Miss Timperley.' Jill handed him the notes. 'Her main concern is that her leg will be disfigured, will never look the same again.'

'Well, it won't, will it? She'll have a scar, that's inevitable. That gash only just missed her artery, so she's a lucky young woman. If the artery had been severed and she'd not been pulled out of her car in good time she could well be lying out there in the morgue, instead of tucked up in bed.' He sounded irritated, even cross, but none of this was apparent when he went in to see the patient and talked to her quietly. 'You leg looks ugly at the moment, Miss Timperley, due to the bruising and swelling, as well as a dozen stitches. Once the stitches are out, though, and nature gets to work on the healing process, the scar will daily get less noticeable. Physio-therapy will take care of your muscles and get them in trim again.'

'And that's it, is it?' Miss Timperley stuck out her chin.

'What else would there be?' he enquired.

'Like when can I go home?'

'It's a little early for me to be able to tell you that, but perhaps at the end of the week. We'll have to wait and see.'

She didn't bother to comment on this, but reached for her headpiece and switched on her radio. Jill and Adam went out.

'We get all sorts, don't we?' Adam said in the office.

'We do, and Donald Chance is just leaving, and here's Mr Gardner, if I'm not much mistaken!' exclaimed Jill, and, sure enough, there was Ruth's father in his hairy tweed suit being taken into the ward by Nurse Sibley, after which Donald Chance came out.

The rest of the visitors began to drift in. So did Joe Buckman, for he wanted to check over his appointments for next day. Adam departed in haste to Outpatients— Jill saw him crossing the landing as she stood at the lifts with Ruth and her father—and after they had gone there were two relatives who wanted to see Sister, and had to make do with her.

Robin Law, the anaesthetist, arrived to check the patients for surgery next day. Sister Beck telephoned from her home in Hendon—not, she said, to quiz Jill as to how things were going, but to tell her that she hoped to see her when she had her outpatients appointment at the end of January. She had just rung off when the hospital chaplain called to see Mrs Irons. He was with her for the greater part of the afternoon

'He's so comforting, dear,' she told Jill when she took in her evening paper. 'He doesn't spout a lot of twaddle at me, but he makes me see that I'll be all right whatever happens. . .that I've nothing at all to fear—and now——' she took the paper from Jill and put on her spectacles '—I'd better catch up with the news, and have a go at the crossword.' Jill switched on her bed-rail light, and Mrs Irons settled down to read.

Clive Barnett rang Jill up at Cade House on Friday night, wanting to know if she could go to a dance with him on New Year's Eve. 'It's at the Assembly Rooms,' he said, 'a charity affair—to raise funds for the hospital— and, as you were once one of its nurses, I thought you might like the idea.'

'Why, yes,' she said, 'I *do* like it,' and she was glad Clive had asked her. She would be bound to re-meet a lot of old friends at the dance. She hadn't made any plans for New Year's Eve itself, and Anna had been asked to a party at Welwyn, given by a writer friend.

Several times during the weekend, however, she couldn't help wondering if she would ever get away by Sunday afternoon. There were no less than four critically ill patients in the ward, but Miss Cooper, true to her word, sent in extra help, while Irene Catling, by her own admission, was at her best when rushed. 'It gets my adrenalin flowing,' she told Jill cheerfully on Saturday afternoon at the end of visiting time.

They had one rather difficult patient—Miss Gulliver, the herniotomy. At only two days post-op, she was threatening to discharge herself. Adam came up to see her, and spent some time with her. 'I think I've persuaded her to stay,' he said, looking in on Jill, who was on the phone to Medical Records, trying to track down some notes. There was a tea-tray on the end of her desk, but she'd had not had time to pour out, and he did this for her, crossing to the kitchen to fetch a cup for himself. 'I hope you don't mind,' he said, sitting down in the visitor's chair, 'but I'm off to Bexford in a minute or two, and this will help me on my way.'

'Of course I don't mind,' Jill said, hiding her surprise, for he never stopped for tea in the usual way—he'd seemed to scorn the stuff. 'Have a biscuit with it.' She passed him the remains of Miss Pink's Christmas tin, and he took a chocolate wafer, peeling the foil off like skin.

'So, when are *you* off?' He sipped his tea and leaned back in the chair. As he did so she wondered if he had any inkling of the effect he had on her. Not that she was sitting there all of a dither, going red and white in turn, but she wasn't at ease. . .oh, far from it. . .she was on what she could only describe as pleasurable thorns, like a kind of tingling that reached right down to her toes.

'I'm not off till this time tomorrow. . .' She pushed her chair a little further back from the desk and swivelled it to face him '. . .but I don't have to get back till midday on Wednesday. Until then Nurse Catling's in charge.'

'Will you be seeing the New Year in?' Up went one quizzical brow. It was a very mobile brow, that one, with an expressive life of its own.

'Oh, yes,' she told him, 'I always do. This year I'm going to the hospital dance at the Bexford Assembly Rooms. It's actually to raise funds for the hospital. I'm looking forward to it.'

'And are you going with one of your old flames from the hospital?' he asked. His eyes were teasing, but he was waiting for an answer. Nosy devil, she thought.

'No. I'm going with Clive. . .Clive Barnett, the vet.

He's at a loose end too. His people live in Alnwick, Northumberland, so it's too far for him to get home.'

'Whereabouts in Bexford does he live?'

'Over the surgery. It's a biggish flat, but noisy, of course, being right on the street.'

'It would be.' He was looking at her, and she felt her face going red.

'What about you—are you celebrating?' she heard herself ask.

'Yes, at the Lawleys'—Vanessa's parents. They live a few doors away from my mother. Colonel Lawley, by the way, is one of the Bexford General's main benefactors. You probably heard about him when you were nursing there.'

Adam was stirring sugar into his second cup of tea. He was taking his time about it. Jill watched the spoon going round. But of course—of course. . .*Lawley*, she thought. . .Colonel Lawley of Mountford Lodge. 'Why, he practically kept one wing of the hospital open at one time!' she gasped.

'So I understand.' Adam smiled faintly.

'But I didn't,' Jill went on, 'connect him with Vanessa Lawley, although the name did ring a bell when you introduced me to her at the surgery the other day.'

'Let's hope we all have a jolly time.' Adam sounded as though celebrations of all kinds bored him. What a sceptic he was, thought Jill. 'Is Clive Barnett on your list of marriage possibles?' he asked, taking her by surprise.

'I was once engaged to him, but it fizzled out, quite amicably,' she said, deciding to be as direct as he was, 'and now we're simply friends. Clive asked me to marry him a few weeks after my parents were killed. I said yes too quickly. It wasn't really the time for decisions like that. But I wanted to be secure and. . .'

'Safe?' Adam supplied.

'Yes, I did, and Clive was there. Clive was like a rock.

He helped me in all sorts of ways. I shall never forget what he did.'

Adam nodded, saying nothing, and she couldn't read his expression. He was looking thoughtfully down at his cup as he put it back on the tray. Jill found herself waiting, found herself holding her breath for his next remark, but when it came it was disappointing, for all he said was, 'I must go—the roads will be chock-a-block,' and with that he got to his feet. He came to the desk, though, and held out his hand, and his smile warmed her through. 'Happy New Year, Jill, and may it bring you everything you want.'

'I wish you the same,' she said formally, but it was difficult to speak, with her hand in his and the whole of her being going into overdrive. She was held in thrall by the intensity of his gaze, by his deep blue eyes—speaking eyes—that were surely, weren't they, sending out messages?

'Goodbye for now.' He dropped her hand.

'Goodbye, Adam; all the best.'

He nodded and made for the door, just as it opened to admit Rachael Marks, who had come in for the tray. Suitable greetings were exchanged with her, and then he went swiftly off.

'Gorgeous, isn't he?' Rachael sighed. 'Isn't he just. . .brilliant?'

With her back to the room as she drew down the blind over the darkening window, Jill agreed that he was, and managed to laugh, to hide what she felt inside.

At eight o'clock on Monday, New Year's Eve, she and her grandmother left Homewood—she with Clive in his car, Anna driving herself to Old Welwyn, while Barney could be seen poking his muzzle through the sitting-room curtains and looking disconsolate.

'I wish we were going out for a meal, then on to a

disco,' Clive said, braking at the lights behind a silver Jag.

'The charity dance was your idea.' Jill, in a wild-silk dress of cherry-red, with a swirling skirt, was already in party mood. 'You know most of the local females,' she teased. 'You'll charm them out of their shoes.'

'I'd sooner charm you out of yours.' Clive was seldom short of a slick answer, yet underneath all his surface patter dwelled a serious man, as Jill knew only too well. He should be married, she thought; he's the type to be married, but then, she supposed, so was she. The thing was, you couldn't just *do* it, not with just anyone. She thought of Adam, who forswore marriage, and his jutting, hard-boned face hung in front of her eyes for a second, like a swinging pendulum.

The first part of the evening passed pleasantly enough, with *no* warning of what was to happen just before ten o'clock. Jill was dancing with Bill Forrest, an old colleague from the General, when someone tapped her on the shoulder to tell her that Clive had collapsed in a heap on the floor, just outside the Gents'. 'We managed to drag him as far as there.' Her informant, a young medical student, had been joined by another, and they were both grinning. 'He's out for the count!' they said.

'If you mean drunk, that's not possible: Clive's teetotal—he was on tonics!' Jill's voice was shrill as her alarm mounted. . .whatever was all this about?

Bill Forrest was guiding her towards the doors, the two young medics following. 'He must be ill—he can't be drunk!' She broke into a run. The doors at last, the cloakrooms at last, and there was Clive lying motionless by the wall, turned over on to his side. They knelt down beside him, and Bill pulled up his eyelids, while Jill felt for his pulse.

'Well, he's drunk all right, no mistake about that, and

if he doesn't drink then someone must have slipped something into his glass.'

'Did you. . .was it you. . .just for some silly joke?' Jill rounded on the two students.

'Steady on, love!' Bill Forrest put a restraining hand on her arm.

'No, it wasn't us, but we saw it done,' the younger of the two boys said. 'Two slugs of vodka went in. We just hung about for the results!'

'Well, I hope you got your money's worth!' Even Bill was angry now. Jill looked at him, then down at Clive.

'I shall have to get him home. His car's on the park; I can drive it. . .I've not had a drink as yet. I must get him back to his flat, Bill, and quietly back as well. It won't do his reputation much good to be seen flat out like this, not even on New Year's Eve.' Jill chewed on her underlip.

'It won't, I agree.' Bill knew Clive was a vet. He also knew that at one time he and Jill had been engaged. 'I'll come as well, help with the lifting, and you,' he looked at the students, 'can tag along and do your bit. It'll help make up for being so irresponsible as to stand by and let it go on.'

'We carried him out here,' the elder one defended.

'Good, then you'll be in practice. OK, Jill, go and get your coat, and we'll do the rest.'

'I suppose he *is* all right?' Jill queried as she drove Clive's Vauxhall off the car park and out into the street. Bill was beside her, the two medics in the back, supporting a now mumbling Clive.

Bill nodded. He was a short bullish man and he still looked belligerent. 'He couldn't have known what hit him. It's virtually impossible to detect the taste of vodka in tonic. It's a puerile thing to do.'

'He hadn't had much to eat either.' Jill steered carefully past a group of revellers spilling out into the road.

He was on call as from midnight—she remembered him telling her that. I just hope no one rings through, she thought, and sent up a little prayer as she drew into the driveway beside his surgery.

His keys had been in his pocket, and it wasn't all that difficult to find the one that opened the street door leading up to his flat. Getting him out of the car and up the steep stairs was the worst. Anything less than three strong men couldn't have managed it. Jill watched the little procession manoeuvring slowly up.

Clive was laid on his bed, his clothes loosened, a duvet flung over him. He mumbled and muttered, seeming to protest, very like a patient surfacing from an anaesthetic, but he very soon slept again.

'He'll be OK in the morning,' Bill said as they all left the flat.

Jill nodded, as though in agreement, but while she drove back to the dance she made up her mind to drop the others off, and then return to Clive. In no way could she bring herself to leave him alone all night. Anything could happen—he could get up and feel dizzy, go to the bathroom and fall, even fall on the landing, or fall down the stairs. So, when Bill Forrest waited for her to get out of the car on the Assembly Rooms car park, she sat still and shook her head. 'I'm going back to him, Bill. . .to stay with him. . .to make sure he's all right.'

'He *will* be, Jill; he won't be hung over. Vodka seldom has that effect.' Bill peered in at her under the roof, shivering in the wind.

'Even so, I'd rather be there.'

'Isn't that hard on you? You'll miss the best part of the evening, when it comes up to twelve o'clock.'

'I can do without the "auld acquaintance" routine,' she laughed, then thanked him for helping with Clive. The two young medics had quickly scarpered inside.

'Well, if you're sure.' He stood back from the car.

'Quite sure, Bill.' They exchanged New Year greetings, then she rolled up the window, reversed and
turned, and drove swiftly back to Clive.

He was still asleep—she could hear him snoring as she
climbed the stairs to the flat. She looked in on him. . .he
hadn't stirred—and, going into the sitting-room, she
decided to spend the night on the couch, but first a
blanket, she thought. She certainly didn't intend to sleep
in Anna's gorgeous Italian shawl, loaned to her for the
night.

In the airing cupboard, however, she found treasure
in the shape of another duvet. . .manna from heaven,
she thought. Folding it round her, she went to the
window and looked down into the street. In another half-
hour it would be midnight; she might as well wait up for
that. Besides, she would have to ring Anna and tell her
where she was. Anna would be back around half-twelve,
for that was the time they had arranged to drink their
own toast to the newly-born year, raising their glasses to
the framed photograph of Jill's parents up on the mantelshelf. Oh, damn Clive, she thought, or rather damn
whoever doctored his drink. Going to the fridge, she
found some Coke, and, taking it back to her seat by the
window, she waited for midnight to strike.

There was little motorised traffic, but plenty of pas-
sers-by. Pedestrians of all types, some in evening clothes,
were moving along the pavements in couples and small
crowds. There was giggling and laughter, outbursts of
singing, and someone shouted 'Belt up!'. A very much
under-the-influence man was sagging at the knees
between two girls who were trying to hold him up. But
when midnight struck, when the bells pealed out from
St Peter's Church on the hill, a cheer went up, followed
by a vociferous rendering of 'Auld Lang Syne'. Jill sang
it under her breath.

Anna was in when she rang through to Homewood

half an hour later. 'I can understand you staying,' she said, 'but what a bind for you, and how will you get home—in the morning, I mean?'

'I'm sure Clive will drive me; he'll owe me that much—not that he could help what happened.'

'Of course he couldn't.' There was a small pause, then Anna said, 'Look, I'll fetch you, that's the best way—I don't *need* to lie in. So, when you're ready in the morning, ring me. In the meantime, my love, a happy New Year. Now, get some rest, or try to, at any rate. I'm absolutely dead on my feet, and I dare say you are too.'

Jill was, but sleep eluded her until nearly five a.m. Clive's couch wasn't all that comfortable, and her dress kept riding up underneath the duvet, and most of the time, of course, she was on the listen for Clive, for supposing he rolled off the bed? But from five until nine she slept dreamlessly, and she might not have surfaced then if Clive hadn't woken her—a bewildered Clive, asking what had happened, asking why she was there, looking down in blank amazement at his clothes. . .and also at hers. She told him all of it, she told him the lot, leaving nothing out. He was furious, but then, who wouldn't have been? 'Damn whoever it was to hell!'

'The thing is, how do you feel?' she asked out of a sandpaper throat.

'Not too bad—nothing that tea and aspirins won't cure,' he said. His expression changed as he looked at her. 'Fancy you staying with me! I never thought that would happen again.' Gently he moved a strand of hair away from her sleep-flushed face.

'I was afraid you'd fall and break your neck.' She got to her feet, pushing the duvet back on the couch. 'I'll go and make us some tea.'

'*I'll* make it,' he said, and she let him. He'd come to by degrees, she knew. She went to the bathroom and sluiced her face, then joined him in the kitchen, Anna's shawl pulled tightly round her for warmth.

'Did many people witness my fall from grace?' Clive asked.

Jill shook her head. 'I'm sure not. Bill Forrest was very good. He's discreet, so you needn't worry, and the two young medics won't dare to blab, or they'll have him to answer to.'

'I can begin to remember bits of it now. Bill asked you to dance, and I went to the bar, ordered a tonic and stood there, looking on. My glass was on the counter—that must have been when it was doused. I drank it down quickly—I was thirsty—and I said how bitter it was. I can remember gales of laughter and my legs packing up, then absolutely nothing else till I heard a lot of singing. . .I was here on my bed then, I knew I was, but I couldn't be bothered to rouse, or move a finger—it was as though I'd been drugged.'

'When you've showered and changed you'll feel fine, Clive.'

'I don't feel too bad now.'

They drank tea from tall mugs, sitting on stools in the kitchen, and Jill was just about to ring Anna when the phone shrilled, making her jump. Clive went on to the landing to answer it. 'Clive Barnett.' His voice was crisp, and Jill marvelled at this, for, in spite of the tea, she felt very unlike herself. There was something particularly decadent about sleeping in one's dress. She fingered the material. She longed for a bath, she longed to get home; then Clive appeared in the doorway. 'I've got to get moving,' he said. 'The Greersons are bringing their cat round—it's been having fits again.'

'Good *lord!*' Jill stared at him.

'Don't worry, I can cope.' He made tracks for the bathroom, and presently she heard the dash of water, the buzz of his shaver, the lesser sound of him cleaning his teeth.

He could cope all right, that was obvious, but it wasn't what she had meant. He knew it too; for Clive was no fool. 'Don't worry,' he said, returning to the kitchen in jeans and a shirt, 'your secret is safe with me!' His hair was damp, and he smelled freshly of soap as he bent and kissed her head. 'I know you fancy the handsome Adam and want to stand well with him. Cast-off boyfriends know these things; they can recognise the signs.'

'That's not true!'

'Which part's not true?' He grinned, then became alert as he heard a car and clattered downstairs to open the surgery door.

Distinctly, as she stood there, Jill heard Adam's voice, then Mrs Greerson's, both becoming muted as the inner door was closed. Going through to the sitting-room and looking down into the street, she could see Adam's red Lotus, see the sun gleaming on its roof. Of all the patients to come here this morning, it would have to be *that cat*! Poor old thing—she spared it some sympathy, then thought of herself again. Clive was right, of course; she didn't want Adam to know she'd been here all night. It would look as though she'd lied when she'd told him Clive was all in her past. So I must keep out of sight— cloak and dagger stuff, she thought. And now I'll ring Anna. She did so, practically whispering down the phone. 'Can you come in about twenty minutes, Anna. . .? Yes, Clive seems quite all right; he's downstairs with a patient at the moment. . .yes, he had an early call.'

Anna asked how *she* was, and Jill assured her she was fine. 'A bit woolly-headed, but that will pass. I'm longing to get home!'

They rang off, and soon afterwards a car door slammed

below. Looking out, concealed by the curtain, Jill saw the Lotus move off.

'They've gone.' Clive came upstairs again, pulling off his white coat.

'How was the cat?'

'I sedated him; there wasn't much more I could do. He's already on Mysoline t.d.s., to keep his fits under control. Mrs Greerson thinks the world of him, and so does your current heart-throb—Adam, the dashing registrar!'

Jill let that pass. 'Anna's coming to fetch me—I rang her,' she said.

'I'd have driven you. . .I intended to.' They were through in the kitchen again. Clive had his back to Jill, slicing bread for toast.

'You're on call,' she said, 'and it's all right, Anna doesn't mind.'

'OK if that's the way you want it. I'm grateful to you, you know, for what you did for me last night. I loved having you here.'

'You didn't know I *was* here,' she told him with point.

'Neither I did. What a criminal waste!' They both laughed at that, but Jill felt a shade uncomfortable, and knew she was glad, even relieved, when she heard a car drawing up.

'That'll be her. . .that'll be Anna! Bye, Clive, take care!' Gathering her shawl about her, and picking up her bag, she went down the stairs fairly slowly, mindful of her high heels. There was no need to break her neck, was there. . .not right at the start of the year?

She was rocked back on those same heels, however, when she opened the street door and stepped out into the biting wind, for Anna's car wasn't in view. Instead, Adam's Lotus stood at the kerb. He was sitting behind the wheel, while his mother was trying the surgery door and walking inside. Within seconds she was out, plainly jubilant, brandishing some gloves. 'It's all right, I've found them—they *were* there!' she called out to Adam, who was looking at Jill standing there in her red evening gown, her shawl slipping down from one shoulder, her hair blowing wild in the wind.

Mrs Greerson, who had not recognised her at first, suddenly did so, explaining that she had missed her gloves, and thought they might be back at the surgery. . .'And so they were—I'm so glad, I didn't want to lose them.'

She moved round the front of the car and got in it, while Adam said, through the open window, smiling rigidly at Jill, 'If you're waiting for a taxi I should do so inside, or you'll catch pneumonia.'

'I'm not,' she said, but he didn't hear her, as he was pulling away from the kerb. Mrs Greerson was talking to him, her face turned his way—that much Jill saw before the car accelerated from view.

She did as he had said, and went inside, but only to call up to Clive to remind him to lock the surgery door. A minute later Anna's Renault hove into sight. And yes, it really *was* her this time. Teeth chattering, Jill got in beside her. 'I'm glad you've come.'

'Well, of course I've come; didn't I say I would?' Anna reversed into Clive's driveway, then turned towards Windon, driving slowly down to the lights. 'And whatever were you doing standing there with the door wide open? I'd have rung the bell.' She was warmly clad in a sheepskin jacket, her soft hair chignoned above its collar, her face discreetly made up.

'I thought it was you a moment ago, when a car drew up,' Jill said. 'I didn't bother to go upstairs again, that's all.' She didn't want to explain about Adam; she didn't feel she could. What she wanted to do was forget the whole incident, to dismiss it from her mind, but she

found this difficult—in fact, impossible—and the
memory of Adam's face, stiffly smiling and hard-eyed,
framed in the car window, continued to haunt her on
and off all that day.

CHAPTER SEVEN

ANNA had won a box of chocolate liqueurs at her party, and early on Wednesday morning she gave these to Jill to take back to town. 'At my age, darling, chocolates are out, tempted though I am. You'll do me a favour by taking them out of my sight.'

'The nurses will love them—we've just about cleared the Christmas goodies,' said Jill. She was right too; they were hailed with delight, especially by Irene Catling.

'I'm fat already, so I've nothing to spoil.' She popped one into her mouth before going into the ward to tidy beds.

Miss Enid Gulliver, so Dick Lane told Jill, had thought better of walking out. 'But with luck we may be able to discharge her officially tomorrow. She's been a bit of a trial, hasn't she?' He glanced towards her bed. Miss Gulliver had refused breakfast, but was tucking into biscuits, shaking the crumbs from her sheet down on to the floor.

Mrs Irons was to be transferred to a hospice as soon as there was a vacancy. Jill was upset to hear this, but could see that it had to be. She would get good care there, specialist care, and, quite apart from that, she shouldn't be blocking a surgical bed when the waiting list was so long.

There was a new learner nurse, Fay Martin, and Jill took her with her when she prepped the first patient for surgery—there were eight listed for that day. 'This patient, Mrs Lomas, is suffering from appendicular dyspepsia,' she explained. 'She's not an emergency, but she needs her appendix excised to cure her symptoms.

Now we're going to have to shave her, and swab her abdomen with antiseptic. We shall need sterile towels, dressing forceps, cotton-wool swabs, scissors and a razor. Oh, and a gown and a cap for her hair. After we've prepped her and checked her over it'll be time for her pre-med.'

It was a busy morning, but operation days were always the worst. As one patient came back from Theatres, another was wheeled down. Jill snatched a cup of coffee between pre-medding a vagotomy patient, and attending to the phlebotomist, who had lost the name label off a specimen jar. Joe arrived to give Mrs Leaming breathing exercises, the laundry manager came up hotfoot to complain about some sheets. There was no time, not even five minutes, to dwell on personal problems, not that Jill needed to do so, for during yesterday she had decided that when the opportunity presented itself she was going to tell Adam exactly why she had been at Clive's flat all night. She didn't *have* to explain, she just wanted to do so, but the timing had to be right. For instance, she couldn't just grab him, could she, and blurt it out pell-mell? But, basically, he was reasonable; he would listen to her, she was sure. All she had to do was pick her moment, and sort of filter it through.

Anna Stevens's view was—for Jill had eventually told her about the episode—that it would be best to leave things as they were and not make an issue of it. 'The truth will emerge eventually,' she had said, but Jill wasn't so sure. Anyway, she had made up her mind; she was going to clear the air.

It was annoying, in the middle of an action-packed morning, to return to the office after the SNO's ward-round to find Enid Gulliver with her fingers dug into Anna's box of liqueurs. But Jill's annoyance changed to alarm when she saw the half-eaten top layer. None of the nurses had been dipping in, they hadn't had time to do so, and even the 'addicted' Irene Catling had only succumbed to one.

'You'll be ill. . .they're rich. . .and you had no business to be in here!' Jill's voice rose sharply. A nurse should never harangue a patient, but this really was too much!

Miss Gulliver looked mutinous as she shuffled her slippered feet. 'I like a walk round—there's no harm in that; the doctor said I should walk round. Anyway, I came in to see you about going home tomorrow. The chocolates were just lying there; I didn't think you'd grudge one.'

'So you ate a dozen!'

Miss Gulliver said nothing. Jill took her back to bed, and asked Nurse Bell to give her a dose of mist mag trisil. 'Now just lie there quietly, please, Miss Gulliver; it'll help your digestion to cope.'

'I've never had any trouble that way, apart from my hernia.' She still looked mutinous, but swallowed the white liquid down.

Jill worried about her on and off during the rest of the morning, unfortunately not without cause, for, just after one o'clock, Enid Gulliver, having refused lunch, started being violently ill. To be sick was horrible at any time, but when you were only six days post-op, and when your stitches were dragging, the result was agony, and poor Miss Gulliver—in spite of the fact that she'd brought the whole business on herself—elicited the sympathy of all the nurses, who supported her through it, holding her scar area, and laying her down flat. But it was when Jill was sponging her face that the worst news came out— Enid, exhausted and spent, said she thought something had split. . .

'It's my wound, Staff; I can feel it wet, as though something's trickling out!'

Jill's eyes met Nurse Catling's on the other side of the

bed, each mirroring the other's alarm, which was very quickly concealed. 'It may be nothing much, Miss Gulliver,' they folded the bedclothes back, 'but we'd better look, hadn't we?' As Jill lifted the woman's nightdress she saw what she had dreaded—a seeping dressing lying over the curved scar in her groin.

Shaking her head at Nurse Catling, who made to undo the dressing, she covered Miss Gulliver up again, reassuring her as much as she could. 'It looks as though you may have loosened a stitch—perhaps when you were straining just now. We'll get Doctor up to look. Just lie still and try not to move.'

'She's Mr Greerson's patient,' Nurse Catling said as they moved away.

'I know that.'

'He won't be pleased.'

'I know that too.' Icy fingers stroked Jill's back. There'd be hell to pay about this. 'Get Switchboard to bleep Mr Greerson,' she told a gaping Nurse Bell, 'then lay up a dressings trolley and bring it into the ward. I think it's likely that the theatre staff will have broken for lunch, so Mr Greerson and Dick Lane will be in the dining-room.'

Jill's face showed none of the worry she felt, showed nothing of the turmoil inside her. She longed for Sister's presence, longed with all her heart not to be the one in charge. . .not to be responsible for everything that happened on the ward. She went back to the patient and sat by her. 'Don't worry,' she said, 'I'll stay with you till Doctor comes—you're going to be all right.'

A step sounded outside the drawn curtains. It was Adam, she could see his shoes, then the whole of him as he moved the curtains on one side with a single swish. She got to her feet and explained what had happened. He nodded, then smiled at the patient. Jill took the dressings trolley from Nurse Bell and aligned it close to the bed.

'Now what have you been doing, Miss Gulliver?' Adam asked as he put on his mask. After donning hers, and gloves as well, Jill exposed Miss Gulliver's wound. It was as she had thought, as she had feared. Once the gauze was removed, a layer of raw flesh met their eyes, the remnants of stitches clinging to the skin on either side.

Adam bent to it. Only skin and muscle were affected; he saw that at once. It was a lesser degree of burst, but, damn it, he thought, it shouldn't have happened at all. 'There's a little bit of damage, Miss Gulliver, but nothing we can't put right, and put right easily, so don't you worry yourself.' He signalled to Jill to lay a sterile towel over the wound. 'What we're going to do is get you back to Theatre for a minor repair. Now, it won't be a long job, and we won't have to put you to sleep this time. You'll have a local, you won't feel a thing, and before you know where you are you'll be back here again, safely back in the ward.'

'It was all my fault,' Enid quavered, looking up at him. She was still very frightened; she was paying very dearly for her greed.

'We won't go into whose fault it was.' Adam's gaze passed from her to Jill, who knew exactly what he was thinking and who he was blaming too. 'How could you,' he asked her out in the office, where he was ringing down to Theatre, 'have been no thoughtless. . .so *careless* as to leave those chocolates about, in full view of anyone who might be passing the door?' He glared at them— they were still on the desk—and Jill put them away in a drawer.

'They were left out for the nurses,' she said, raising her eyes to his. 'I didn't expect a patient to come in; they very rarely do.'

'That's scarcely an answer, is it?' He was speaking to Theatres, asking them to get ready to receive a patient for secondary suture. 'Yes, I'm doing it myself—yes, in about ten minutes!' He put the phone down very gently and carefully, then looked at her again. 'I said that's scarcely an answer.' His blue eyes were flint. If he'd given her time she'd have said she was sorry, for she *was* responsible, but he went on talking rapidly, snappily, giving her no space. 'You should have put that box of *sweets* out of sight.' He made them sound like poison. 'Anything can happen when a patient is ambulant and inquisitive as well. You've been nursing for long enough to realise that.'

'Yes, I have, but Adam——'

'Mr Greerson, please. . .we're both on duty.'

Jill went white. She could feel the blood draining from her face; she felt as though she'd been shot.

'Send her down to Theatres in ten minutes' time.' His eyes avoided hers. 'I don't want the afternoon list affected.'

'No, of course not,' she said, out of a throat that was rapidly closing up.

Adam went off very quickly without a backward glance, and soon after that Miss Gulliver was wheeled down to Theatres. She was allowed glucose and water only for the rest of the day, but next day she was eating normally, grumbling about the food and about having to stay in hospital for another three or four days.

As for Jill, she had learned a hard lesson from her brush with Adam. He had been angry and upset about Miss Gulliver, and this she could understand, but surely he needn't have been quite so rude, quite so cutting and snubbing? She couldn't forget how smartly he had pulled her up over his name.

But her unhappiness was her own fault, and she knew that very well. She had allowed herself, in a very short time, to care what he thought about her. . .to like him too much. . .to want to please him. . .to want to stand well in his eyes. In that sort of situation one was a sitting target for hurt. Well, she might not be able to rectify that—at least, not at once—but with practice she could, and intended to do so, by keeping distance between them. She should never had shortened that distance in the first place. She had allowed herself to be beguiled by him, but not any more. She would grow a second skin.

During the next few days, therefore, she made a passable job of protecting herself behind a shield of smiling pleasantness. Everything went smoothly on the ward, Miss Gulliver was discharged, and as Jill was crossing the landing after seeing her off she was waylaid by Adam, who stopped her and remarked on how well she was managing. 'It couldn't have been easy having to take up the reins from Sister Beck,' he finished a little uncertainly.

'It wasn't, but I'm enjoying it,' she replied, remembering not to show blazing pleasure at his words, but to accept them as her due. They parted company at the corridor doors, for he was going to Male Surgical. Jill smiled a goodbye and sailed through to Ecclestone, leaving him standing there for the minute it took to watch her go, then he plunged through to Charlestone Ward.

It was almost a fortnight before she was on days off again, and then whom should she see in the books department of the Bexford store but Mrs Elaine Greerson. She had her back to Jill, who instantly recognised that upright figure in a belted raincoat and matching hat, and soft suede boots. She had taken a book down from one of the shelves, a sizeable book on cats— Jill could see the cover from where she was standing, see the white cat on its front. Glancing at the paperbacks, and deciding not to make herself known, Jill presently saw her making her way towards the escalators. Well, she wouldn't be joining her son, for he was on call this weekend. Perhaps she was meeting the smooth Vanessa and having coffee at Dawsons. Anyone or anything to do with Adam still intrigued her, of course. She wasn't cured yet, but she was getting there. I'm not made of marshmallow, she thought.

Out in the street ten minutes later, she saw Mrs Greerson again, standing in a knot of people waiting to cross the road. They were watching the crossing lights; the red man was still showing, but one or two of the more intrepid shoppers were crossing anyway, including—Jill saw with a thread of alarm—Mrs Greerson herself. Now that was foolish. She was Anna's age, and no longer fleet of foot. No sooner had Jill thought this than she saw a small van all but hit her, shaving so close that she overbalanced and fell. There were gasps from the crowd, a screeching of brakes, the lights changed and the traffic halted. The crowd swirled over the road, Jill among them. By the time she reached Elaine Greerson she had got to her feet, and was on the opposite pavement, being handed her shopping-bag by a woman with a baby on her hip. Seeing her white face and shaking hands, Jill led her straight into Boots and to a row of chairs inside the doors.

'Are you all right, Mrs Greerson? Do you feel any pain? It's Jill Arbor—I saw you fall.'

'I'm perfectly all right.' She was defensive at first, then admitted, as she tried to rise, to feeling dizzy. 'It's the shock, I expect. I was silly to. . .to dash like that.'

'I'll run you home.' Jill made up her mind quickly, on the instant. 'It's not very pleasant being toppled like that. I've got my grandmother's car in the car park here, just at the rear of the shop.'

Mrs Greerson inclined her head in assent, and, holding her arm, Jill got her through the shop, out to the car park and into the car. 'You live in Mountford Drive, don't you?'

'Number twenty-four.' A tear rolled down Elaine's cheek, hastily disguised and mopped up together with a trumpeting into her handkerchief. 'So silly of me!'

'Not at all, you've had a nasty experience.'

'I just followed those other people, you know. I wasn't looking at the lights.'

'I saw you.' Jill turned out of the High Street and was passing St Peter's Church. Hill Avenue lay to the right, and Mountford Drive was a turning off it—a tree-lined road of elegant houses set back in their own grounds.

Number twenty-four was low-slung, with white walls and a green roof. A conservatory bulged out from one side, and a monkey-puzzle tree stretched intricate pine-needled arms over the front lawn. Jill pulled up at the grass verge outside. 'May I see you in?' she asked, getting out and opening the passenger door, taking Elaine's basket and bag. It was then that she saw the blood on her ankle. 'Doesn't that hurt?' she exclaimed.

'A little, yes; it's stuck to my stocking. I didn't notice it at first.'

'You'd better let me have a look at it, hadn't you? I'm a nurse, remember,' Jill pressed gently, for quite possibly there were other grazes as well.

'Well, perhaps. . .yes. That's very kind.' Elaine Greerson gave in at last. 'I have a housekeeper, but she's out today. If you'll hand me my bag I'll find the key.' She was still very shaky, and Jill kept a hand under her elbow as they went up to the front door.

The hall smelled of polish and chrysanthemums and faintly of coffee. It was a square hall with a curving staircase and an alcove at the back, where they left their coats, and in a downstairs cloakroom suitably equipped with vanitory wash-basin Jill bathed Elaine Greerson's leg.

'It's only a graze; it'll just be sore.' She examined it carefully. 'It's what's rather unsympathetically called a superficial wound. . .in hospital circles, that is.' She tore open a packet of Inadine and bandaged it over the wound. 'You're so right to keep a first-aid box in the house.'

'I'm not so foolish as a rule.'

'I'm sure you're not.'

'But my cat died last weekend. It's had quite an effect on me. I can't seem to get over the loss.'

So *that* was it, thought Jill. Poor woman, no wonder she was distressed! Mrs Greerson was pulling up her stocking, her eyes downcast. Jill knew she was going to have to be careful not to say the wrong thing. She would never forgive her if she made her lose her composure all over again. 'That's dreadful!' She shut the first-aid box and replaced it on the shelf. She took her time about this, not turning round till she heard Mrs Greerson enquire if she would like a cup of coffee.

'That is, if you've got the time, Miss Arbor.' She was very dignified.

'Why, thank you, yes, I'd love one.' Jill tried not to sound surprised.

'It won't take long. Mrs Parkes will have left it ready to heat. I could smell it when we came in.'

'Can't *I* bring it through? Jill offered as they came out into the hall.

'You're my guest, and I'm not an invalid,' was Elaine Greerson's reply as she showed Jill into a patio room overlooking the garden. A living-flame gas fire flickered in the grate, two leather armchairs placed on either side of it, while the opposite wall was given over to books, the shelves climbing nearly dado-high. A kneehole desk flowing with papers and a modern sewing-machine on a separate table took up most of the other available wall.

Left on her own, Jill glanced at the books, seeing

Anna's among them, a whole row, vying with those of Dick Francis on the shelf below. There were classics as well—Sir Walter Scott, and the Herries Chronicles.

'This is my workroom,' Mrs Greerson said, coming in with the tray. 'I do my sewing in here, and my committee typing. Adam calls it my den. As you see, I'm a reader, always have been. Adam was, too, as a boy. Now he gets very little time for it.' She began to pour out the coffee. 'I'm so looking forward to your grandmother's new book.' She smiled over at her guest.

'The hardback came out last week,' Jill said. 'Anna was in Mapletons, St Albans, most of Thursday, signing and promoting it.'

'How thrilling!'

'Yes.'

'Is she working on another?'

'Practically *finishing* another, but that won't be out for a year at least. The time lag between finishing a book and seeing it in print is very long indeed.'

'How interesting,' Elaine Greerson murmured. 'Fascinating, in fact. And what about Mrs Stevens's little dog? Does he keep her company, in her study, when she's working, I mean?'

'Anna works in the dining-room, and when Barney fidgets it drives her mad,' Jill laughed, 'but on the whole they understand one another, wear each other well.'

And from then on, as she had rather expected, their talk led to Seamus. It was, she felt, good for Mrs Greerson to get the whole thing off her chest. 'In the end the fits affected his heart,' Elaine explained, 'and he died last Sunday morning. I rang your friend Mr Barnett, and he came at once, even though Seamus was dead, and he knew he could do nothing for him. He couldn't have been more kind. He took Seamus away, rolled in his blanket, and later came back to make sure I was all right and help me dispose of his things. Mrs Parkes was here, but was good for nothing, except wringing her hands and saying, "Oh, my good lor. . .!", which didn't help very much.'

'I can see that it wouldn't,' Jill said, visualising the scene.

'Adam came as soon as he could, which was late that afternoon. He rang Mr Barnett to thank him—he always does the right thing.'

'Yes, I'm sure he does.' The biscuit Jill was eating caught in her throat, and she choked a little swallowing a mouthful of coffee to help it down.

There was more talk after that—about animals in general—then Jill, hearing the clock strike eleven, made movements to go. She had promised to be home by midday and she still had some shopping to do. As for Mrs Greerson, she was looking much better; her colour had returned, and she appeared to be more in command of her legs when she saw Jill out to the car. 'Thank you,' she said, extending her hand and shaking Jill's warmly. 'A little help's worth a load of pity, as my father used to say.'

Jill smiled and eased into the driving seat. 'I was glad to help,' she said.

'And you're the only person, other than Adam, who hasn't *annoyed* me by asking if I'm going to get another cat.'

Which she will in time, I'm quite sure, Jill thought as she drove away, even though, right now, the idea appals her, which is very natural. Perhaps Adam and I share the same kind of carefulness about people and their reactions. Perhaps we're both tactful, or do I mean wary? Then, furious with herself for coupling herself with him in *any* way, she deliberately brought her thoughts to bear on her shopping, and what she was going to do with the rest of her day.

CHAPTER EIGHT

JILL was on lates on Tuesday, arriving on the ward just after midday to find three patients back from Theatre, another on her way down, two more being prepped, three others awaiting their turn, and two new ones being admitted and settled into their beds. It was the usual non-stop operation day, and she certainly didn't expect any of the surgeons, other than Dick, to visit the ward.

At six in the evening, however, she was at the ward desk, writing the report for the SNO and keeping an eye on the beds of patients who had visitors, when June Sibley came in to tell her that Adam was in the office and wanted a word with her.

'He wouldn't come into the ward, Staff, he's dressed for going home. He said he wouldn't keep you a minute.' She smoothed down the front of her dress, looking self-conscious. What an effect that man has on us all, thought Jill.

'Thank you, June.' She got up from the desk, aware of nervousness. Had she made some kind of slip and sent a patient down to Theatres without her ID band, or without her X-rays, or with her dentures still in? She knew she hadn't, for these things were always rigorously checked—a 'cockpit check', Sister had used to call it. So what had he come about? She was near enough to the viewing window now to see him sitting there in Sister's chair, the light from the desk lamp gilding his brown-red hair. He saw her pass, and when she entered the office he was already on his feet, his anorak hanging loosely from his shoulders, the collar rucked up at the back.

'Ah, Jill, come in!' As she did so he shut the door behind her. He didn't sit down or suggest she should do so. 'I won't keep you long,' he said, 'but I just wanted to thank you for what you did for my mother on Saturday. I was able to get home for a few hours yesterday and she told me all about it.'

'It was nothing—I was glad to help.' Relieved, Jill smiled at him.

'I'm afraid poor old Seamus's passing has affected her badly.'

'I realised that, and I'm sorry about it. How's her ankle going on?'

'Healing well; it's no longer so sore.'

'I'm glad,' Jill replied. There was silence for a few seconds, then, when they eventually spoke, it was together, they clashed words, and both apologised. They laughed too, but even that didn't ease the atmosphere, which was the strained kind, making small sounds loud, making breathing difficult.

'Well, anyway,' Adam took a package out of his pocket, 'she asked me to give you this, as a small way of saying thanks.'

'Oh, how nice of her!' Jill took it from him. It was wrapped and in a box. She was nervous and nearly dropped it.

'Don't worry, it's not a bomb,' she heard him say as he brushed past to the door.

'Please thank Mrs Greerson for me.' Expecting him to go out, she was surprised when he retraced his steps and sat on the edge of the desk, extending his feet and legs over the carpet, very close to hers.

'It's a paperweight,' he said, 'one of those snowstorm things. Open it, see if you like it.'

She did so, hurrying, feeling all thumbs, seeming to see the border of his anorak cutting across his legs even more plainly than the globe-shaped paperweight, which she presently held on her palm. 'Oh, its beautiful—thank you!' It showed a man and a girl tobogganing down a slope.

'Don't thank me, it's from my mother,' She fancied he sounded amused.

'Then I'll ring her up.'

'She'd appreciate that.' He moved, and she saw his hand gripping the edge of the desk. He didn't seem to be going, and Jill found herself holding her breath. It was impossible to speak, impossible to move; she couldn't even manage to invert the little glass paper-weight to make the snow drift down on the man and girl holding fast to the sides of their sleigh. I'm not proof against him, and I never will be—that truth came home to her with zinging force as she heard him say, 'There's something else that I ought to mention.'

'Oh, really?' She swallowed hard.

'Yes, a letter,' he said, 'from Ruth Gardner,' He produced it and shook it out with one hand. 'She and Donald Chance are getting married on the twenty-third of February, and they want us to go to the wedding. They seem to think that if it weren't for us they'd both be dead. . .they're nothing if not dramatic! The wedding is at St Martin's Church, Seftonbridge, and there's a buffet luncheon at the University Arms Hotel. They're doing it in style.'

'Good heavens!' Jill stared at him.

'Amazing, isn't it? Here you are, see for yourself.' Adam passed the letter to her, and she scanned the scrawled sentences, trying to take them in.

Ruth was feeling fine, but wouldn't be returning to her flat in Highgate, nor to her job, which was why she was asking for her Outpatients appointment to be switched to the Seftonbridge General. . .'My father says this can be done'. She and Don were looking forward to their marriage, and were buying a house at Ely. . .'Don's

father is finding him a job in his boat-building firm'.
More details followed about the wedding. Ruth was
clearly over the moon, and once more, towards the end
of the letter, her voice seemed to leap from the paper.

> Please try to come, and bring the staff nurse called
> Jill, who talked me through my bad times. My parents
> will be writing formally, but this is a pre-notice, as
> Don and I know how busy you are, cutting people up.

'She makes you sound like Sweeney Todd!' Jill handed
the letter back. 'It's a very nice gesture. . .asking us.'
'Exactly! So, what do you say?'
'I'm not sure.' Jill went to the window and stood
looking out into the lamplit darkness, trying to make up
her mind. Should she go with him. . .*should* she? Her
heart leapt at the thought, but common sense was a
damper, and it also spoke the truth. If you go, Jill Arbor,
you'll be undoing all the good you've done over almost
the past three weeks; you'll be losing ground again.
You'll draw closer to him, you'll give yourself away, he'll
see that you're keen on him. You'll be in his power and
it'll be impossible for you to work with him on the ward.
Even now it's not easy, but it's possible, because you've
drawn back from the brink. You must keep your distance, or you'll make a fool of yourself.
She turned round to find him facing her way, plainly
waiting for an answer. Ruth's letter was sticking out of
his pocket, she could see the pale blue edge. 'It's sweet
of Ruth to ask me as well,' she began, 'but I don't think
I can go. I. . .I do have something else on that particular
Saturday.'
'Can't you put it off?' His face darkened and she felt
that he knew she was making excuses. She shook her
head.
'No. . .I can't put it off.'
'I see—well, that's that, isn't it?' He picked up the

paperweight and shook it, and the snowflakes all but fizzed. Jill stared at them, then heard him say, a little more equably, 'I shall go—I'm keen to. As a university town, Seftonbridge holds happy memories for me. I read medicine at St Mary's but haven't been back for some time. I shall probably make a weekend of it, and revisit one or two old haunts.'

'Sounds like a good idea.' Jill tried to sound as if she meant this.

'It does, doesn't it?' And he looked, she thought, delighted at the prospect. He was even humming under his breath as he opened the door and went out, treating her to a wide smile before he passed from view. Jill had a feeling of anticlimax, almost of affront. He was glad she'd refused to go with him, that much was obvious. He'd had to go through the motions and ask her because Ruth had invited her, but, having done so, he was cock-a-hoop, and hadn't been able to hide it. Most likely he was planning to take Vanessa to Seftonbridge; most likely, right at this moment, he was winging his way over to the Barbican flat to put the whole thing to her. There would be plenty to amuse Vanessa in Seftonbridge while Adam was at the wedding. He was making a weekend of it, he'd said as much. It didn't really take much imagination, did it, to fill in all the blanks?

She looked at the little glass paperweight Mrs Greerson had sent her. She shook it and watched the snowflakes whirl, then put it back in its box, and not for the first time she wondered if it might be a good idea for her to apply for a transfer to another part of the Walbrook. She would have to wait until Sister was back before even making enquiries, but if she was ever to get over Adam— if that was the right phrase to use—she would have to move to a part of the hospital not visited by him, like, for instance, Paediatrics, or the neurological wing. It *could* be done. . .it wasn't impossible. . .All is not lost, she thought philosophically, and began to feel better at once.

During the following few weeks relations between them were uneventful, and smooth enough, but not without strain for Jill. She was much more at home with Sir Rodney, for instance, who always sang her praises, and with Dick, who teased her and was more of a friend. . .they still had the odd evening out together, steering clear of abandoned bikes.

There was a completely new set of patients in the ward, most of them abdominal cases. Mrs Irons, who still hadn't been transferred to a hospice, was the only 'old friend' left. Her ascites, as Adam had known it would, had gradually built up again, and, although she managed, with help, to get out of bed most days, she couldn't walk more than a step or two, and eventually the day came when Sir Rodney and Adam decided to try the effect of an epidural to relieve her discomfort and pain. As this proved to be successful, it was made more permanent by the injection of phenol into the spinal theca, which effectively blocked the nerves sending the pain messages to her brain. After this she was bedfast, but was cheerfully disposed, and felt well enough to take more notice of what went on around her in the ward. Whenever she could, Jill sat down to talk, or read to her. Mostly this was in her off-duty times, which Rose Irons looked forward to, as, although she had a son, he could only visit at weekends.

'I lost my husband when we were both very young,' she told Jill one day. 'I had a chance to marry again, but decided not to take it. Sometimes I wish I had, but it's too late to think of that now.' She smiled almost roguishly, her teeth starting out from her face. 'Still, there's plenty of time for you, dear.' She touched the fob watch on Jill's dress. 'If you get the chance of a good man, take him, snap him up, or someone else will; you can bet your sweet life on that.'

Jill thought of Clive—a good man, if ever there was one. If she'd married Clive they might have had two or three children by now. She might have been nursing part-time at the Bexford General. But she hadn't married Clive, had she, because she had ended the engagement? She hadn't loved him enough, or in the right way. He had said he understood, but it had split them forever, or so it had seemed, then after a year had elapsed Anna had come to live at Homewood, Barney had needed veterinary care, Clive had provided it, so Jill and he had met again in that way, met again with all rancour gone, met again as friends. And that is the way it will always be; one can't love to order, Jill thought a little sadly as Mrs Irons touched her hand.

'What day is it, Jill?' she enquired.

'Wednesday the twentieth of February.'

'Getting on.'

'Yes, getting on.' And Saturday would be the day when Ruth Gardner and Donald Chance would marry, when Adam would attend their wedding, and join up with Vanessa afterwards, probably staying the weekend in a plush hotel. Jill shut her mind on that thought.

'It's nearly spring,' Mrs Irons was saying.

Jill smiled at her. 'Yes, it is. At home, in my grandmother's garden, we've got daffodils in bud. Some of the trees are filming green, and the birds are pairing up. . .' even the birds had love-lives '. . .they think it's spring,' she said.

'An early spring. . .the birds always know.' Rose Irons's eyes were closing. After a few minutes Jill got up and left her, calling out 'Goodnight' to Irene Catling as she went up the corridor.

When she went on duty at eight next morning it was to learn from Night Sister Paul that Rose Irons had passed into a coma at midnight and died at three a.m. It had been expected; everyone had known that she couldn't live much longer. She herself had been happy to go, and had said so many times. 'An early spring. . .the birds always know.' Those must have been her last words. Jill felt low, sick at heart, when she saw Rose's stripped-down bed. She kept her feelings under wraps, though, for nurses always did. It was hardly therapeutic for the rest of the patients—some of them very ill—to see a grieving nurse's face. It was quite bad enough that most of them knew what had happened; they needed to be reassured, and talked through it; they needed their fears put at rest.

Dick said all the right things to Jill when he came to do his round. Adam was absent; he was operating at St Mildred's, as Sir Rodney had a cold. 'She didn't have to leave us to go to the hospice; she stayed with us to the end.' Dick took Mrs Irons's notes out of the cabinet and laid them on Jill's desk. 'She looked upon us all as friends, Jilly, especially you.'

'I hope so,' Jill said hoarsely, just as Joe Buckman came in. Joe wasn't unfeeling, but he was given to platitudes. Phrases like 'happy release'. . .'much better for her'. . .'now she's at rest' tripped off his tongue as though they'd been used many times before. But he gave Jill's hand a squeeze as he said them, and offered to take Mrs Irons's notes down to Medical Records when he left the ward.

The ward-round proceeded as usual, Jill escorting Dick, while down in Admissions arrangements were being put in hand to contact a Miss Martin of Hackney Downs who would fill Mrs Irons's bed.

Jill's feeling of depression persisted throughout the rest of the day. She wasn't sorry when four-thirty came and she was able to go off duty. She felt stifled in the overheated building, and it was good to get out into the cool evening air. She breathed in great gulps of it as she made to cross the courtyard, then suddenly changed her mind and sat down on one of the wooden seats, huddled in her cape.

It wouldn't be dark for another hour; the evenings were drawing out. A purple crocus was thrusting up between the flags at her feet. The sight of it, its fragile perfection, proved to be too much. Tears spilled out of her eyes and dripped down on to her hands. She couldn't stop them, and she didn't try to—there was no one there to see. She wept because of Rose Irons, there was no doubting that, but she also—and she knew this to be true—wept for herself; she wept out of a terrible loneliness.

And a fat lot of good it'll do you, she told herself presently. What on earth's the use of tears? They've never cured anything as yet. She was so busy diving for a tissue in her bag that she didn't hear Adam approach. He had spotted her on the seat as he had come down the steps from Cas. As he drew nearer he saw her distress, and thought he knew its source. Dick Lane had told him about Rose Irons in the rest-room earlier. 'You'd probably rather be left alone, but at least let me give you this,' he said, standing in front of her and offering his handkerchief.

Jill gave him a startled, angry glance, and all but snatched it from him. 'Thanks—I don't seem to have one.' She blew her nose like a man, mopped her face, and decided against saying she'd got a cold. He wouldn't believe her, his eyes were all-seeing; she couldn't even plead a bad case of hay fever, not in February.

She wished he would go, but he seemed to have changed his mind about doing so, for, although he moved, the shift of the seat told her he was sitting down. Her face burned and she felt a mess. She heard him cross his legs, then said so quietly that it was almost under his breath, 'Hospital life and all its trauma has a way of getting under the most hardened of skins at times, and the effect can be shattering.'

She hated the fact that he'd seen her upset, and her voice had an edge as she said, 'Nurses are supposed to be detached.'

'So are doctors and surgeons. They're also expected to be human beings, which means they have to care. Caring and detachment don't make good bedfellows, Jill.'

'No, they don't. She raised her face and let the breeze cool her cheeks. He was motionless beside her; she could see the curl of his hand as it lay on his knee. He was conveying sympathy and understanding by simply sitting there. She was grateful for his silence; she was filled with feeling, the sort she dared not analyse, the sort of feeling that made her want to do things for him. . .*all* things for him. . .anything he asked.

'Of course,' he said as they got up to go—he was on his way to Pathology—'you could improve *my* lot at a stroke simply by coming to Ruth Gardener's wedding on Saturday.'

'The *wedding*?' Jill's voice rose, 'but surely,' she said, 'surely you've long since made all your arrangements for that?'

'Not absolutely,' he was quick to explain. 'I've accepted for myself. I told the Gardners that you'd like to come, but might not be free to do so. They said not to worry, but if you *could* come then I was to bring you. The reception is a buffet affair, so seating won't be a problem.'

'So I can still come?' She met his eyes.

'I wish you would,' he said. 'It'd do us both a power of good to have a little fun.'

'It's Nurse Catling's turn to do Saturday.'

'Well, then, you've no excuse.'

'I can't think of one,' she retorted, and then they both

started to laugh. The tensions of the day rolled away, Adam drew nearer and touched her hair.

'I'm glad you've changed your mind,' he said. 'I didn't think you would. I thought you were determined to make me go to Seftonbridge on my own.'

'I thought you were going to spend the weekend there.'

'I decided against it.' He broke off as he saw the long figure of Dr Cragg approaching. 'See you tomorrow about the arrangements. Don't change your mind again.'

'No chance!' she laughed, and, stopping only to acknowledge Dr Cragg, she rose from the seat and made her way to Cade House.

CHAPTER NINE

JILL had thought that Ruth Gardner would be one of those trendy brides, with a bouncy dress above the knees and a neckline that plunged. Not so. Ruth was traditional in white satin and a veil. She had two little bridesmaids in rose-pink, while the lanky Donald, who again Jill had thought would arrive in his Levi's, was skinnily tall in a light grey suit that fitted him like a glove.

Standing beside Adam in the crowded church on Market Hill, Seftonbridge, hearing his ringing baritone voice partnering her own in the wedding hymn, 'O perfect love', Jill was glad she had come. Just for one day, just for this day, I can let down my guard, she thought.

'Dearly beloved. . .' the vicar intoned. The service had begun.

Later, at the reception, as they were served delectable food from the buffet her light-hearted holiday mood prevailed. She and Adam sat down at one of the many tables provided. Champagne flowed, guests ate and drank, the noise level was high. Then came silence for the speeches, and the bride and groom were toasted. People promenaded from table to table, and the happy couple, together with their respective parents, came to talk to Adam and Jill.

'If it hadn't been for you two we wouldn't have been here today,' Ruth said dramatically, while Donald Chance put his arm round his wife's waist and said,

'That's right.'

'He's learning fast,' Adam said, after they'd passed on.

'In what way?' Jill chased a blob of whipped cream round her plate.

'To agree with his wife.'

'And that's good, is it?'

'Saves argument, and rows.'

'Dull, though.'

'Agreed,' he laughed, then sobered and said. 'You look beautiful, Jill.'

'So you said in the train coming down.'

'You look more so now.'

'That's the wedding ambience getting to you.'

'Not entirely,' he said. His eyes passed over the jacket of her wine velvet suit, with its nipped-in waist and upstanding collar, and matching pillbox hat. He noted the gleaming bell of her hair, the spiky fringe that gave her a slightly gamine look, and his gaze lingered on her mouth.

'I feel as though I'm on holiday.' She lifted her glass and drank from it, wishing he wouldn't stare at her quite so hard.

'I wish we were.' He was flirting now, and making her blush and be glad to be joined by a doctor from the hospital, who introduced himself, saying that he'd heard what excellent care Ruth had received at the Walbrook. 'Compliments from all sides,' said Adam after the man had passed on to talk to an Indian girl in a sari with hair that reached her waist.

'The Walbrook enjoys a fine reputation, but then, so does the Bexford General.' Jill felt she had to praise her old hospital.

'So I understand.' Adam shifted his chair a shade nearer hers. 'Speaking of which, you and I have a mutual friend at the Bexford General.'

'Do we?' Jill's brows rose. Who could that be? she wondered.

'Bill Forrest. . .Dr Bill Forrest.'

'Oh, I know Bill well!' she exclaimed.

'So he told me when I met him in Bexford a fortnight ago. We had a drink together, and we got on to the subject of that *dangerous* practice crass idiots have of doctoring unsuspecting people's drinks.'

'Oh, I see.'

Immediately he said that Jill knew what was coming next, or thought she did, and was proved to be right, for he went on to say, 'He told me that someone did that to Clive Barnett on New Year's Eve. . .that the poor chap became legless and had to be taken home.'

'Bill and I took him home,' said Jill, looking straight back at Adam. 'I stayed with Clive until morning. . .which I think you already know. I was worried about him, in case he tried to get out of bed and fell. There's a steep flight of stairs running down from his flat, with nothing to stop a headlong tumble. Anyway, I stayed.'

'You don't have to explain.' Adam's eyes held amusement, or Jill thought they did. She felt angry with herself for *bothering* to explain.

'Well, I know that!' she snapped. 'It's entirely my business and——'

'None of mine,' he finished quietly—so quietly and good-humouredly that she felt a touch of remorse.

'Sorry to be so touchy.'

'Think nothing of it.' He smiled then added more seriously, still holding her eyes. 'Perhaps you're still in love with Barnett, as he is with you.'

Jill shook her head. 'You're wrong on both counts. I'm not, and he's not—love doesn't come into it. We care about one another, though. I'd always help Clive if I could, and if I got into some sort of fix he'd do the same for me.'

'Sounds ideal.'

'Well, in that sense it is.'

'You're a caring person, Jill.' He encircled her wrist as it lay on the table, and she didn't pull away.

'I'd better be caring—I'm a nurse, remember?' She smiled wryly at him.

'I'm unlikely to forget.' His thumb moved over the soft inside of her wrist. . .forward and back. . .little gentle movements, mesmeric movements that made her head swim, that made her long for him.

It was a relief and yet an intrusion when another couple joined them, the talk became general and light-hearted, as befitted the wedding scene. It was a full hour before Jill and Adam had a chance to be together. 'So. . .how are you doing?' he asked, whispering in her ear. They were standing, because they'd been going round, talking to various groups.

'I've drunk too much wine and I'm thirsty.'

'Champagne has that effect. Once the bride and groom have left and we can politely do the same, shall we have a pot of tea somewhere before we get our train?'

'I can't think of anything I'd like more,' she said, just as Mrs Gardner brought more people up to be introduced, and once again it was nearly another hour before—with the bride and groom waved off—Jill and Adam could reasonably say goodbye and leave the hotel.

A fine drizzle of rain was falling as they stood on the steps, but they had come prepared with light nylon macs. Jill's had a hood, which she pulled up over her pillbox hat. 'Pity it has to be like this.' Adam frowned up at the sky. 'Does it put you off?'

'Not in the least. I'm not letting you off that promise you made to me about tea.'

'Right, then, off we go.' They began to cross the road, he holding her arm and weaving her in and out of the traffic in a manner that left her breathless.

'It's worse than London!' she gasped.

'The streets are narrower, the congestion greater,' he

said as they bent their heads to the fine rain and walked
through to Princes Parade.

Jill stood and admired. It was different here; the road
was wider, more grand, lined with colleges on one side,
élite offices on the other, interspersed with little bow-
fronted cafés and restaurants.

Adam took her to the Copper Bowl, pulling her up
two flights of stairs to the big square tea-room with its
magnificent view of St Saviour's College and Chapel, and
a glimpse of the river beyond. The Parade itself was
awash with traffic, mainly bicycles, the latter ridden with
such lack of care that Jill couldn't bear to look at them.
Adam laughed when he saw her wince.

'Cyclists are a feature here.'

'Yes, I know, but the risks they take.'

'Students bear charmed lives.' The waitress appeared
and he ordered tea and toast which, rather to Jill's
surprise, she found she was hungry enough to tuck into
when it finally arrived.

He told her a little about Seftonbridge, about the town
and its surrounds, about the rivers that linked upland
and lowland, about the dykes and the outlying Fens. He
was good at description, and she listened, enthralled,
watching the different expressions flitting across his lean
face, watching his eyes deepen in colour, watching his
hands, the tips of his teeth when he smiled.

The time passed, and he looked at his watch. 'Our
train doesn't leave until six, which gives us another clear
hour,' he said as he refilled their cups. 'Shall we drink
up, brave the rain, and walk across to the Backs? I could
show you my old college, not to mention the crocuses.
People come from miles to see Seftonbridge crocuses.'

'OK, fine,' she agreed, as airily as she could. She'd
have walked the length and breadth of Seftonbridge with
him if he'd wished—walked it in darkness, in pouring
rain, hail and a howling blizzard—but she wasn't going

to let him know this, for how craven it would have seemed. And, apart from that, remember Vanessa, her common-sense voice warned. . .you've only got him today, you know, tomorrow he'll be back with her.

The rain was nothing but a fine mist when they left the Copper Bowl. Most offices and cafés had switched on their lights, which was how Jill's eye was drawn to an attractive bow window displaying a Queen Anne chest, and nothing else but catalogues scattered around its feet. The catalogues had 'Rothenby's' scrawled on their covers, and the same name in gold lettering above the shop window. 'I didn't know Rothenby's had a branch here!' She peered through the window, seeing a group of men inside looking at something on a stand.

'Oh, yes, they have four branches in England,' Adam's voice came from behind her shoulder, 'and also one in New York. Vanessa—Vanessa Lawley—is one of their auctioneers. She's in Brussels this weekend on some kind of road-show affair. Her speciality is paintings; she's very knowledgeable.'

'How interesting!' Jill flashed him a smile as they walked on again. But it was strange how the finely honed magic of the afternoon seemed to dull, strange how the mist became rain and got inside her mac, how the breeze became a nuisance and blew her hood back off her hat. *If Vanessa hadn't been in Brussels this weekend he'd have brought her to Seftonbridge, he wouldn't have asked me—re-asked me—right at the very last minute. She'd have come with him and visited Rothenby's while he was at the wedding, and then spent the weekend with him at a hotel.*

She was quiet as they crossed the Parade on to the college side, passing through an archway into an open courtyard. Her heels clicked on the flagstones and echoed angrily back from the walls. She felt cross both with him and herself. She should have refused to come when he'd asked her the second time, for whatever was the point of allowing herself to spend more time with him, and fall deeper and deeper in love? For she did love him, she acknowledged that; she loved him utterly. She had loved him since Christmas, when they'd sung together and he'd kissed her for the first time. She shivered, and he felt her do so.

'Are you all right?' he asked. 'You're not regretting this, are you. . .you're not getting too wet?' He let go of her arm and reached for her hand. Ungloved, it curled within his, and every resolution she had made collapsed like a pack of cards.

'I don't mind the rain, and I'm not regretting a single thing,' she said. It was a rash, even an inviting declaration to make. Adam pulled her closer.

'You're a sweet girl.' He turned her round to face him. 'But your hood has slipped its moorings; we can't have that.' He drew it carefully forward, tied it under her chin, then bent and kissed her smiling mouth, smoothing the rain from her skin.

Arms about one another, they passed through a second arch, which brought them out to the riverbank and the backs of the colleges. The fine rain misted the view, and they saw it through the veil—the college buildings rising up from the saturated lawns, bridges appearing as grey ghosts, giant beeches dripping moisture from dark branches, the famous crocuses refusing to show more than streaks of colour, keeping their petals furled.

Further along, on the opposite bank, Adam pointed out his old college—a long white balustraded building set amongst gaunt trees. 'What a pity we can't cross the bridge and look at it closer to.'

Jill began to step forward, but halted when he said, 'Anything over the other side is college property. In any case,' he drew her back under the sheltering trees, 'we ought to be making tracks, you know, if we're going to get that train.'

'I suppose so.'

'You sound reluctant.'

'I am—I don't want to go.'

They looked at one another, their eyes locked and Jill felt her legs go weak. His eyes were so blue, and she seemed. . .she seemed to be drowning in their depths. 'Do you think I do?' His voice became urgent, and he gripped her upper arms. 'For God's sake, *do you think I do?*' He snatched her up to him, unbuttoning her mac, unbuttoning her jacket, moving his arms round her back, his hands caressing her, moving downwards, 'I want to make love to you.'

'Oh, Adam, yes——' Her words were cut off as his mouth fastened on hers, as the movements of his hands became all there was. I shall love him till I die, was the last coherent thought in her head before she gave herself up to the surge of delight that left room for nothing else.

'Will   you   stay   with   me   here. . .in Seftonbridge. . .tonight?' His words were a blur in her ear, and so close that she felt they were in her own head and that she had spoken them. Leaning back in his arms, she looked at his face and saw the question still there in his eyes. But she also saw the world again—the grass, and the trees, and the rain; she smelt damp leaves, felt the breeze on her cheeks, felt a return of caution and sense. He wanted her, and that was wonderful. . .wonderful. But he didn't love her too. He just wanted her, which meant a very short happiness—here and then quickly gone, a pleasurable incident; that was all it would mean to him. I couldn't bear to part with him afterwards. . .it'd just be a one-night stand. And somehow or other the much-used and very ugly words gave her the impetus and strength of mind to shake her head and make a joke about the after-effects of champagne.

'I'm not used to it. . .and I'm sorry. . .I know I led you to think. . .' She dried up then, she couldn't say any more, and she couldn't see his expression. His face was in shadow above hers, but she felt the jolt he gave, his abrupt movement away from her.

'In that case, fasten your coat, and let's be on our way.' He didn't sound angry, merely distant. He was turning up his collar, thrusting his hands deep in his pockets, waiting patiently for her as with trembling fingers she tried to do as he said.

They set off side by side, running some of the way, for the rain had thickened and was blowing straight at them. Jill felt miserable. I handled it so badly, I behaved so badly, that he'll never, ever forgive me. He was angry now, she could feel it—feel it in the touch of his hand on her arm as they crossed the Parade and made for the taxi rank.

In the taxi, going up to the station, she sat upright on the seat, bracing herself not to roll against him, making herself respond to his comments on the places of interest he was pointing out to her. He was still the attentive, courteous host, but that was all he was. No one, but no one would ever have guessed that half an hour ago they had been locked in one another's arms, lost to the outside world.

The diesel train drawing in from Ipswich was nearly full. Adam found a seat for Jill, but had to stand himself. His upright position in the centre of the aisle and her sitting-down one weren't conducive to conversation, which was a respite for both of them.

More people got on at Martley Halt, and Adam helped a young girl with her case. She was clearly very taken with him, swaying there beside him in skinny black tights and leather jacket, flicking back her hair. He needed to do very little to attract the opposite sex. All he had to do was *stand* there. Tearing her eyes from his tall, lean figure, Jill turned her head window-wards. Darkness had fallen as fast as her spirits, and the sight of her troubled reflection did little to cheer her. She closed her eyes and feigned sleep.

Adam was at her side promptly when they got out at Liverpool Street. 'We'll probably have to queue for a taxi,' he remarked on their way to the barrier. 'I'm assuming you're coming back to the hospital and not going down to Windon?'

'You assume right,' she told him, and they exchanged wary smiles. Jill felt microscopically happier. At least he still likes me, she thought childishly, resisting the urge to slip her hand through his arm.

During the short taxi ride down Broad Street, across Moorgate to London Wall, their conversation was forced and sporadic, but kept going to a certain extent by their driver, who was one of the chatty sort.

'Thank you for coming with me, Jill,' Adam said formally when they reached Cade House and stood at the foot of the steps. He was looking intently at her, and she felt he was about to say something else—something important that might have made things better. But he backed away as a gust of wind blew coldly between them. . .like an ill omen, Jill thought sadly, stumbling up the steps.

CHAPTER TEN

THE main item of news when Jill went on duty at midday on Monday was that Sister Beck would be back on duty as from the fourth of March.

'Next Monday. . .oh, that's terrific!' she exclaimed. Irene Catling shrugged.

'Which means I'll be leaving you, I expect.'

'But perhaps not at once. I should imagine that Sister will be able to do with an extra pair of hands for a week or two,' Jill said more slowly, not knowing if this was the case. 'You've been great, Irene. I couldn't have coped without you here.'

'I like being here; I like the ward.' Irene Catling shrugged again. 'Anyway, to bring you up to date, we've got two new patients in, both for pancreatic surgery, and Miss Cooper suggested that we put them in adjoining beds—they were admitted yesterday. Oh, by the way, how did the wedding go off?' She was adjusting her cap, and not looking round, which was just as well, for to Jill the mere sound of the simple word 'wedding' had the effect of a sharp blow very near her heart.

'It was fine,' she enthused. 'Ruth looked fantastic—a trad bride, all in white. I enjoyed it, so did Adam. . .Mr Greerson. . .and it didn't go on for too long.'

'Mr Greerson would be good company, I imagine.'

'Oh, he was, yes, the best.'

Jill knocked a pencil off the top of the desk, and bent to retrieve it in time to hear Irene Catling say, 'Just as well you brought him back.'

'How do you mean?'

'Well, he wasn't on call, but he volunteered to assist

148

with an accident case. Part of a wall collapsed in Clone Street, and a young woman was buried. She had crush injuries, mainly trunk, and she's in ITU. Three surgeons worked on her—one of her kidneys was excised.'

'What age?'

'Young. . .still in her thirties.'

'How awful,' Jill said.

'Awful, I agree, but it could have been worse.' Adam strolled into the office, giving both young women a start, for they hadn't heard him approach. Jill's heart leapt in her throat; she felt for the back of a chair and hung on to it, bracing her legs, which had gone to rubber foam. 'It could have been worse,' Adam repeated, 'if she hadn't been promptly dug out by two brawny types who'd just finished a night's drinking at the Goldsmith Arms. Have you recently come on duty, or are you off to lunch?' he enquired of Jill, turning a bland face in her direction.

'I've had my lunch,' she told him. 'Nurse Catling's just going for hers, so if you want to see. . .'

'I do want to see,' his chin gave the merest jerk, 'the two new patients, in other words, Mrs Beccles and Mrs Tarn. Thank you, Nurse Catling.' He took the notes from her and passed them to Jill. 'You'll have read these, of course?'

'Not yet,' she replied, reacting to his tone. 'We haven't had time for a hand-over yet—apart from the verbal kind.'

Irene went off, pulling a face at Jill behind the door. Senior surgeons had little idea of how nurses go on, she thought. Even dedicated charmers like Mr Greerson need setting straight at times.

In the ward, at the desk, as though glad to escape the closer confines of the office, Adam was opening Mrs Ada Beccles's notes. 'She has what Sir Rodney and I consider to be a harmless tumour,' he said. 'This has developed from the islets cells and is having the effect of producing insulin, giving her hypoglycaemic attacks.'

'Resembling insulin overdose,' Jill said, not quite airing her knowledge, but letting him see she knew exactly what he was talking about.

'Although adenoma of the pancreas is rare,' he continued, 'that's what all the signs indicate.' He closed the notes with a snap. 'She's second on the list for tomorrow. I want Mrs Tarn down first; she's a far more serious case, with an encroaching growth at the head of the pancreas, causing obstructive jaundice. She'll need extensive surgery, and will be a heavy nursing case.'

'Of course.' Jill nodded, and walked with him to the two beds near the ward doors. One was curtained, while, lying on the top of the quilt of the other one, busily knitting, was Mrs Beccles in a scarlet, much frilled nightdress. She had short black hair and dark eyes, and looked just like a poppy. She had already met Adam in Outpatients, and greeted him nervously, dropping her knitting, and rubbing her clammy palms together. Jill felt she could understand the need for the brilliant nightdress. It was a kind of flaunt, a covering-up of what she was feeling inside. It was defiance too, *and* a bonus, for the colour suited her. She was a long-faced, handsome woman of nearly forty-two.

Adam explained what would happen next day, and what he intended to do. 'You'll feel much better afterwards—you'll have no more of those sweating attacks of yours.'

'I dread being cut,' she whispered. 'I've always hated knives.'

'Lots of people feel like that, but you'll know nothing about it,' he promised. 'You won't even have much of a scar—just a little line under your breast. By this time next week you'll be wondering why you worried.'

'Thank you.' She said very little, but patients were

often silent. The mere fact of being in hospital made them feel clammed up. Jill noticed, however, that by the time Adam left her she was looking less tense, and when she started to knit she wasn't quite so frenetic about it, so perhaps her worst fears had been laid to rest.

In the next bed, Mrs Tarn was lying back on her pillows. She was markedly jaundiced, a deep ochre colour, only her teeth gleamed white, which gave her a curious ethnic appearance. She complained of a pain in her back.

'That, too, is due to your pancreas trouble,' Adam explained. He didn't want to have to explain too much— at least not at this stage. 'You'll be my first patient in Theatre tomorrow, so you'll be back before all the others—have a head start on them, in other words.'

'I'd sooner not be in that kind of race, Mr Greerson.'

'I can understand that,' he said, 'but, since you are, you may as well win, which I'm sure you will.'

'Win through, you mean?' Her face was so thin that it made her nose look beaked. She had a skin irritation, which was driving her crazy, but she didn't mention that. So far as she was concerned, the surgeons could do what they liked. She hadn't really been ill for that long, but it seemed to have been forever.

'With help from me,' Adam was saying, 'and effort on your part, combined with good nursing care, you'll win through with flying colours.'

She closed her eyes, disdaining to comment, so, pressing her hand in a farewell gesture, Jill followed Adam back to the desk.

'I shall want a urine specimen from both patients going down to the labs each morning, for amylase estimation,' he said, scribbling in the notes.

'Yes, of course.'

He handed the notes back to her. 'I don't need to see anyone else.' He didn't need her to walk to the doors

with him, either; she could feel him throwing her off as
they made their way down there in the wake of Nurse
Marks, who was wheeling the lunch trolley out. Once
they reached the corridor, after a polite, 'Thanks for
your help,' and the briefest of smiles, delivered sideways,
he was off and away, not hurrying—he never hurried—
but managing to leave infinite distance behind him with
every step he took.

'How did you get on on Saturday?' Rachael asked,
following Jill into the office. 'What was he like to be
with?' She was curious and couldn't hide it. 'I hope he
behaved himself.'

'Impeccably,' Jill made herself laugh, 'and it was a
really super wedding. Ruth sent her love to everyone,
and there'll be some cake coming later on. Now,
Rachael, if you don't shift that trolley we'll have the
kitchen staff complaining.'

'OK, OK, will do, don't worry!' Rachael backed out
as Dick came in to sign the prescriptions.

'How did Saturday go?' he whispered conspiratorially,
making Jill want to lash out.

'It was a good affair and we enjoyed it. . .*thoroughly*,'
she added. But if anyone else asks me that, she thought,
I'll stand on my head and scream! Several others did,
though, including Joe Buckman, who came up to see
Miss Martin, the patient in Mrs Irons's old bed. Joe,
however, didn't seem all that interested in Jill's answer—
he was all for telling her his own news, which was that
his fiancée, Megan, was coming to London to live and
work.

'She's got a post at St Mildred's,' he said. Megan was
a physio, like him. 'She'll live with me in my bedsit in
Camden until we get married, which will be at Easter,
we hope, if everything goes as planned.'

'I'm glad for you, Joe; that's good news.' Jill and he
gripped hands.

'Megan and I, we get on, you know, and that's the main thing. We pull together, think along the same lines. One day we'll have our own private practice, our own set of treatment-rooms. With Meg beside me, nothing's impossible.'

The sky's the limit, in other words. Jill watched Joe's burly figure making its way into the ward, his dark head moving from side to side as he greeted patients he knew. He was happy, on top of the world. She felt a tinge of envy. Imagine how she would feel if, quite suddenly, out of the blue, Adam were to come bursting into the office and tell her that he loved her, beyond all rhyme and reason, and wanted to marry her. I'd feel the way Joe does, only more so, but Adam will never be mine. Even if there were no Vanessa Lawley, he would never see me as other than a short-term girlfriend. What he feels for me isn't deep.

The next few days were hectic ones for the staff on Ecclestone Ward. Mrs Tarn came through surgery well, but complications—not unexpected—of paralytic ileus meant that a Ryle's tube had to be passed. Intermittent suction was needed to keep her stomach empty, while an intravenous infusion was maintained until Friday when, at long last, intestinal movements could be heard.

Mrs Beccles, on the other hand, made good progress right from the start, and by Thursday, once her drain had been shortened and removed, she was back in her scarlet poppy nightie, and looked very pleased with herself. She was considerate of Mrs Tarn, however, and never wearied her with talk, yet somehow or other—perhaps by sheer instinct—they helped one another along. A strong inter-patient bond could develop in hospital. The Beccles-Tarn one was a prime example, and Adam was warm in his praise of Irene Catling for putting the two women side by side.

Where Jill was concerned he was unfailingly cour-

teous, but entirely impersonal. His eyes were veiled
when he looked at her, and, although he often smiled, it
was a movement of lips and teeth only; nothing else was
engaged. Firmly Jill told herself that this simply didn't
matter, but nevertheless, as each day passed and his
attitude didn't soften, she wondered how much longer
she would be able to stick it out.

On Sunday morning, the day before Sister Beck was
due to return, Dick arrived to see a patient, and to give
Jill an item of news. 'Our Adam moved out of the
residence yesterday. . .what do you think about that?
He'll only have a room there now for when he's on call
at night.'

'Where's he moved to?' Jill asked, feigning noncha-
lance. Yet perhaps she knew the answer, perhaps that
was why she wanted to shut her ears to Dick's answer,
perhaps that was why she wanted to shout Oh, just go
away, go away, I don't want to know! He told her, of
course, for he loved to gossip, he loved to be the one to
bring news pristine-fresh from the grapevine. Sensation,
to Dick, was all.

'To the Barbican flat, my love. . .where else?' He gave
her one of his winks. 'He's moved in with his lady
auctioneer, and good luck to him, I say.'

'Yes, good luck to him.' Jill turned to the trolley of
notes. There was a service going on in the day-room—
she could hear the chaplain's metallic voice mournfully
intoning the Lord's Prayer. There was a chorused Amen
afterwards. She managed to smile at Dick as they went
into the ward to see Miss Martin, who was complaining
of pains in her legs.

And amen, she thought a little while later, when Dick
had gone flying off, just about sums it up for me, just
about says it all. With a clear, cold insight shivering
through her like steel, she realised that if she was ever to
get over her love for Adam she would have to move

away, right away, to another hospital. It would be no good merely moving to another part of the Walbrook. Adam, to her, *was* the Walbrook. Adam was everywhere—in the wards, in the corridors, in Casualty, outside in the yard. . .certainly in the car park. Vividly did she remember her first encounter with him on that mountain bike ten weeks ago. I shall have to tell Sister before anything is decided about Irene Catling, she thought. Irene wants to stay here, which is all to the good. Perhaps, just for a time, *I* could work through an agency, once I'm released from here.

She got up to fetch herself a cup of coffee from the kitchen. She drank it in gulps, looking through the window into the ward, looking at the two lines of beds as though seeing them for the first time. . .or the last time. Her head ached and she felt a little sick. Nevertheless, having made her decision, she felt a semblance of peace and resolution filling her. It wasn't the end of the world.

There wasn't exactly a fanfare of trumpets when Sister Beck returned to the ward, but a certain amount of fuss was made, which was certainly her right. At teatime a special cake was sent up from the kitchens, with 'Good Luck' and 'Welcome' piped across its top. All the nurses were given a slice, and ate it when they could. Even Sir Rodney came up to share it, followed shortly by Adam, Dick Lane, and Miss Cooper, the SNO. Jill was summoned to the office while they were there, and personally thanked for helping out and for coping so admirably.

'She's done wonderfully well.' Sister raised her cup, as though drinking Jill's health in tea.

'I second that,' Adam put in, surprising Jill so much that her plate tipped sideways and a sliver of almond icing fell on the floor. He picked it up for her, squinting at the fluff that adhered to it. 'Unfit for human consumption,' he declared, throwing it into the bin with deadly aim, then turning to smile at her. It wasn't a guarded smile either, it was one of his heart-stopping ones—the kind she hadn't seen for nine days, and instantly she felt the familiar quickening of her senses as well as sharp surprise. When the telephone rang she hardly heard it, although Sister's replies to whoever was calling, and her swift glance at Jill, snatched her attention away from Adam, for was the call meant for her?

Sister had half turned her chair round, so her words came over her shoulder. 'Yes, I'll tell her. . .of course, right away. . .oh, dear, yes I understand. . .how bad?. . .yes, yes, of course. . .all right, Doctor, thank you. Goodbye.'

In the second before she turned round again, in the second before she spoke, Jill knew, felt, *smelt* bad news, and was instantly transported back four years to another hospital, to another ward sister, who had been wearing a similar expression as she had quietly broken to her the terrible news that her parents had been killed.

'What is it—what's happened, what is it?' she cried, dimly aware of Sir Rodney and Dick still holding their plates, of Sister getting up, of Adam shifting beside her. . .

'It's your grandmother, Jill. . .' Sister's voice was low '. . .she's been brought into Casualty. She's had an accident at King's Cross Station—tripped and hit her head.'

'Badly? Do you mean, she. . .?' Jill felt sick.

'She has a head injury and she's unconscious. She was with someone else—someone from her publishers, who's down in Casualty now.'

'I can go, can't I?' Jill backed to the door, which was being held open by Adam.

'I'll go with her,' he called to the others, but it was all he could do to keep pace with her as she sped up the corridor, through the doors and down the stairs. . .and down the next flight. . .and down the next flight, through into Casualty.

Casualty looked much as it always did, brightly lit and stark, with rows of patients awaiting treatment, the curved reception desk manned by two clerks, both of whom were talking on the phone. Near the entrance doors an ambulanceman was talking to a red-haired woman clutching a leather bag to her chest.

There was a buzz of activity in one of the cubicles, where two doctors were coming out. Jill instantly recognised Leigh Sheldon, the neuro registrar. She was about to join him when he disappeared back into the cubicle. Adam caught her arm. 'You wait here; I'll see what's going on.'

He was trying to protect her, she knew that, but she fought with him just the same. 'I want to see her. . .I have to know!' His grip tightened on her arm.

'Wait over here.' He took her to the chairs. 'Please, Jill——' he pressed her down, '—leave it to me, *trust* me; I'll be back in a minute or two.'

Perhaps Anna's face was badly injured; perhaps that was what he thought. She watched him pass the desk and make his way to the cubicles. Unable to sit, she got to her feet, and almost immediately was joined by the red-haired woman from the doorway, who approached with her hand outstretched.

'You're Jill Arbor, aren't you?' She was frowning slightly. 'We've met, if you remember, at a publishers' party—you came with your grandmother. I'm her editor, Delia Shaw.'

'Yes, I remember.' Jill took her hand, then looked beyond her bush of curly auburn hair to the line of cubicles.

'I was with her just now,' Delia Shaw continued, 'when she fell, I mean. This is her bag.' She handed it over. Jill looked at her properly then.

'What exactly happened, Mrs Shaw? Was she pushed by the crowd?'

'No, she tripped and fell, hit her head on the corner of a metal trolley. We'd just got out of our taxi and she was running for her train, which was about to pull out. She quite literally streaked away from me. I was about to make my way to my own platform—I go on the Hertford line—when I saw her fall, pitch forward, and when I got to her she was unconscious, didn't seem to be breathing. I was frantic, of course. Someone called an ambulance, which came very quickly, and they gave her oxygen. They thought, as she was lying near a trolley, that she'd struck her head on that.' Delia Shaw's eyes followed Jill's to the cubicles.

'Thanks for looking after her,' she heard Jill say, and wasn't surprised when she saw her make her way to the cubicles.

Anna Stevens was lying on a stretcher trolley in a semi-prone position. Her face was drained of colour, her chignoned hair was neat, her eyes were closed, and over one eyebrow was a massive raised bruise. Leigh Sheldon, Adam and a staff nurse were with her, and when they saw Jill they called her in. Leigh Sheldon stayed to talk to her, while Adam and the staff nurse went out.

'We've run the usual coma tests,' Jill was told. 'I consider that she's suffering from what we term moderate concussion. Now, as I'm sure you know. . .' Leigh Sheldon was rather a pompous man '. . .that means she's unlikely to be conscious for several hours yet. Until that happens I can't investigate her condition further.'

'But there's no fracture, and you don't think her depth of coma is great?' Jill prayed that he'd shake his head to both questions, which he did, so promptly that some of her anxiety and fear began to take itself off.

'She's going along to the neuro ward now, and once

she's settled in you can sit with her, if you wish to do so. I'm sure Sister Vine won't mind.'

'I'd like to sit with her until she's conscious, however long it takes,' Jill said firmly, moving reluctantly out of the cubicle. The porters wanted to come in, and still waiting around in Reception was Delia Shaw. Remembering her manners, Jill went to speak to her.

'Thank you again for coming, and for all you did, Mrs Shaw. I'm very grateful.' Smiling was difficult, like pushing back doors, but somehow she managed it.

'How is she?'

'In a coma, but they don't think very deep. It's difficult to assess a head injury, though, and caution is always applied.' Jill sounded like a textbrook, and knew it; she wished Delia would go.

'Poor Anna!' Delia Shaw swung her shoulder-bag into place. 'Is there anything else I can do?' she asked, her eyes moving to the clock. It was exactly five-thirty, and if she was going to get the six-ten from King's Cross she ought to be making a move now, but on the other hand. . .

'There's nothing, truly, but thanks again.' Jill walked with her to the doors.

'I'll ring in the morning, just to ask how she is.'

'You can reach me on Ecclestone Ward.'

'I'll do that. I'm so sorry, Jill.' Tying her headscarf under her chin, Delia Shaw ran thankfully into the yard.

Adam caught up with Jill in the covered way that led through to Neuro. 'Are you all right?' he asked. He fell into step beside her, and, worried though she was, the sight of him brought a little warmth to her shock-frozen state.

'I'm all right, yes,' she told him, 'but I'm staying in Neuro until Anna comes round. I want to see exactly how she is.'

'It may be hours, Jill.'

'I shall still wait.'

'You'll need to break and have a meal.'

'I'm full of cake and tea at the moment!' She tried to laugh and failed. What an age it seemed since they'd all been in Sister's office, making speeches.

'Have you thought of the situation at Homewood? Will Mrs Stevens have left everything secure, and what about her dog?' Adam was guiding her past a porter trundling an empty bed.

'Barney will be with Mrs Legge, our cleaner. She always has him when Anna's out. She'll have been at the house when Anna left, so she'll have locked up all right. The only thing is,' Jill's brows drew together, 'she won't want to have Barney for long. She's got a cat, and she'll have to keep them apart, not easy in a small house. Oh, I know,' her face cleared, 'I'll get in touch with Clive. . .I'll ring Clive; he'll take Barney! Oh, what a good thing you mentioned it!'

'Would you like me to ring him?' Adam enquired.

'No, I'll do it from the ward. I'll have to ask him to collect Barney, and everything. I'd better do it myself.'

'Just as you like,' he said agreeably. They had reached the Neuro corridor, and as they walked down it they could see Sister Vine and Leigh Sheldon talking together. As they drew abreast of them Sister greeted Jill and took her into the ward, to Anna's bed halfway up on the left-hand side.

'I understand you want to stay,' she said briskly. She was a small round woman with a gimlet eye that missed nothing. She watched Adam fetching a chair.

'Yes, I do, I want to sit with her,' Jill stated, 'that is, if I may,' she added rather more diplomatically in the face of Sister's stare.

'It will help my nurses to have you here,' Sister conceded. She remembered Jill and Adam from their singing on Christmas Eve. If she wondered why Adam was in her ward now she gave no sign of it, just moved flat-footedly off, after making sure that the charts for recording Anna Stevens's obs were at the end of her bed.

Adam went to stand by Jill's chair and the two of them looked at Anna, who was lying on her side, facing them, the bruise over her eye appearing to darken even as they watched it, and although her eyes were closed she didn't look peaceful; there was an aura of disturbance and unrest hanging over her bed. 'She's likely to be confused, even perhaps delirious, when she comes round, you know.' Adam was trying to prepare Jill.

'Yes, I *do* know,' she said, then turned and put her hand on his sleeve. 'I'm sorry to snap, I didn't mean to!'

'I know what you're going through.' His eyes were full of concern for her; his hand on her shoulder was warm. She was immensely comforted; she could describe what she felt no more clearly than that. All she knew was that the feeling stayed with her, even after he had gone from the ward.

Anna's bed was uncurtained, so as to allow for maximum surveillance. Jill could see some of the other patients, most of whom had bandaged heads. There was a girl on skull traction opposite, while a few beds down was a patient in a plaster shell, another in a 'Halo' frame, making her look as though she were wearing a visor, and nurses were tidying beds.

Anna's arm lay outside the coverlet. Jill moved nearer and took her hand. Oh, come on, darling. . .come on, come on. . .wake up and talk to me, she begged silently, but to no avail; the long narrow hand with its polished nails remained lifeless within her own. Automatically Jill felt for her pulse: it was slow, and she knew this meant that Anna's brain, jarred by her fall, was becoming oedematous. This happened with concussion, even moderate concussion, but supposing there were haemorrhages, serious ones. . .supposing Anna was never herself again? But I mustn't think like that, I mustn't, I must be positive—think good thoughts. You'll be all right, Anna, love; all it'll take is time.

She continued to sit there. A nurse brought her in an evening newspaper, but the headlines swam, blurred, in front of her eyes, while around her in the ward one or two visitors trickled in; then suppers were served. A number of patients were hand-fed; several drank through straws. All this Jill saw, but with half her mind as she sat by Anna's bed.

At seven o'clock a junior doctor, who introduced himself as one of Mr Sheldon's team, came to examine Anna, while Sister suggested that this was the time for Jill to go up to supper. She went, unwillingly, practically dragged there by one of the nurses, who kept telling her not to worry, everything was fine. Her remarks, kindly meant, even her smile, jarred on Jill, who managed to spoon down a bowl of soup before she fled back to the ward. She did ring Clive, though. She remembered to do that. He was upset to hear the news and told her that he would go to Mrs Legge's right away, and pick Barney up. 'He'll be all right with me; I'll be glad to have him, for as long as it takes. What about the house? Do you want to me go?' Clive was anxious to help.

'Mrs Stevens is surfacing gradually. Her level of unconsciousness is not so deep.' Sister informed Jill as she sat down at the bedside again. Hope, even a faint excitement, rose in Jill. The time was seven-forty-five. Perhaps in another hour Anna would be round and talking to her, but this wasn't the case. Two and a half more hours passed, and the day shift had changed to the night one before Anna's head moved, before she twitched and opened her eyes.

'Anna, it's me. . .it's Jill, darling! You're in hospital. . .you're all right!' Jill leaned over her, holding her hands. Anna had rolled on her back. The junior night nurse appeared, then the staff nurse, who bleeped Leigh Sheldon. By then it was very apparent that Anna was totally confused. She looked at Jill with hostile eyes, and when one of the nurses tried to make her more comfortable she pushed her away with her hands.

'She may be like this for a day or two,' Leigh Sheldon told Jill out in the office, while in the ward cot-sides were being affixed to Anna's bed as a safety measure, just in case she should roll herself out. 'And I think,' he peered over his glasses at Jill, 'that it would be best if you entrusted your grandmother to us, and went home to bed. You can ring in as early as you like tomorrow, and sit with her again, but not. . .' he turned her firmly away from the wide viewing window '. . .again tonight, for there isn't any point.'

Jill might have argued if Adam hadn't appeared in the corridor, wanting to know if there'd been any change. He was told the details, after which he and Jill took one last look at Anna, who was muttering restlessly, moving her head from side to side, saying something like 'Rose' or 'Rosemary', and 'be a good girl', and 'no, I don't want to go out'.

'Rosemary was my mother's name. Perhaps she thought I was her,' Jill said huskily as they walked up the corridor and entered the covered way.

'She can't think rationally at all at the moment. No one can guess what's going on inside her head.' Adam held fast to Jill's arm.

She kept stumbling—her legs were numb. 'It's awful to see her like that. I know I see patients disorientated every day of the week, but when it's your own, when it's someone you love, it's a very different thing.'

'I know. . .I know. . .I know that!' His voice was as husky as hers. He turned her to him and kissed her hair, and held her for a minute, tenderly yet firmly in his arms. She took strength from his nearness, and comfort came through, and she felt her love for him welling up and, for the first time, was glad that it was there.

They walked on; they were nearing Casualty, where bustle and lights were all. 'I've been to your flat and seen Christabel Anderson,' Adam said, steering her through. 'I've told her she's got to look after you. Ah, here she is now!' And, sure enough, there was Chrissie in her old tartan trousers and Aran jersey that hung in loops, a matter of yards away.

Chrissie said nothing much at all as she hurried Jill up to the flat. She took a good look at her, plied her with milk and whisky, and got her to bed. 'Tomorrow's another day,' she grunted. 'It'll all seem different then.' Then she added, as she put out the light and leaned back into the room, 'He doesn't *just* lust after you. There's more to it that that, and a whole lot more to him that you haven't fathomed yet.'

Jill couldn't fathom anything, not after Chrissie's 'dose', for, try as she might to keep awake, she slid down into sleep.

CHAPTER ELEVEN

OVER the whole of Tuesday and Wednesday Anna Stevens continued to talk at random and to complain of headache. Her irritability subsided, however, and as far as Jill could tell she appeared glad to see her, although she persisted in calling her Rose.

'Perhaps,' Adam suggested, 'you resemble your mother in looks.'

'We had the same type of looks, the same colouring,' Jill said. 'It's quite spooky, though, to have her look at me and see my mother. It's as though I've turned *into* her, as though she had never died.'

Adam nodded reflectively. They were in the office on Ecclestone Ward. He had been called up to see Mrs Tarn and to change her sleeping drug. On the whole Mrs Tarn was doing well and the threatened peritonitis hadn't manifested itself; normal bowel sounds could be heard. She would probably be back on oral feeding before the weekend. All she needed was encouragement to get well, for she was apt to think the worst.

It had helped Jill during the last two days to be busy on the ward, especially physically busy, to be actively employed. She remarked this to Adam. 'But it can't be easy,' he said, marking the way the skin over her cheekbones apeared to be tightly stretched. There were violet shadows under her eyes, but it was the end of the day, of course, and very nearly the end of her shift, for at nine-thirty p.m. the night staff would be coming on duty, when off she would go down to Neuro to talk to her grandmother and hope for a lucid response. 'What shift are you on tomorrow?' he asked her.

165

'Lates,' she replied. 'It's so marvellous to have Sister back—it takes off some of the strain.' She had been going to tell Sister that she wanted to leave, but that would have to wait. Nurse Catling was still with them. because Rachael Marks had flu, so with one nurse short the powers that be had decided to keep Irene on. Jill still intended to leave; she hadn't changed her mind about that. Meantime she looked at Adam going over to the door, and, taking her courage in both hands before he disappeared, said, 'Thank you for being so concerned about Anna, and for being so kind. You've supported me in a way that no one else could.'

He stood stock-still for several seconds, then turned slowly round. 'Do you know, Jill Arbor, that's the nicest thing you've ever said to me?' Clear astonishment rang in his voice and sat in his eyes, which went darkly blue as he approached the desk again. As he leaned across it, palms flat down, the surprise in his eyes gave way to a very different expression. 'But you mustn't,' he said, 'say things like that to a man like me, unless you mean——' He broke off with a curse as his bleep began to sound off in his pocket, as voices in the corridor heralded the arrival of the night staff, and, as if this were not enough to put paid to their conversation, Jill's telephone rang and she moved to answer it. Adam was wanted in Casualty. He went off there at speed, while Jill greeted the night nurses and gave the report, after which she collected her cape, unpinned her cap, and went quietly and thoughtfully down to the neuro ward.

Anna was asleep, and looked so peaceful that Jill felt a change must have come, and this was borne out by the staff nurse going off duty, who told her that her pulse and respiration were less slow. . .

'Which means that the oedema is subsiding, and that has to be good news.'

Even better news was telephoned through to Jill at

Cade House next morning. Anna, although suffering a degree of amnesia, was aware of her surroundings, of who and what she was, and why she was in the Walbrook Hospital. Best of all, she wanted to see her granddaughter.

'The message from her,' Sister Vine intoned over the phone, 'is tell her to come as soon as she can—she can fill in some of my blanks.'

Jill timed her visit until after she knew the doctors would have done their round, which was just after eleven-thirty. She found Anna sitting up. At first they could neither of them say very much; they simply hugged one another, and blinked away tears, or Jill did. Anna was all smiles under her bruise—now a spreading mixture of greenish yellow and black. 'When I saw it,' she said, 'I nearly died, and just look at my hair! As for this nightdress, I think it's been taken out of the drawer marked "shrouds"!'

Jill laughed. 'I'll get your things from home—I'll go tomorrow night. We can talk about that later, but first I want to know how you *feel*—no more headache, I hope?'

'No, but my head's muzzy; it's a job to sort things out. I think of something and then it's gone, and I can't get it back again.'

'It won't always be like that; it's only temporary.'

'But how long is temporary? I'm told I'm suffering from amnesia—I'm sure you know all about that.' Anna's hair had been combed down and plaited. It lay in a single rope over her shoulder. She looks older in bed than when up and dressed, Jill thought. Fancy sprinting after a train at her age, *and* in sling-back shoes!

'Well, without straining, tell me how much you can remember of what happened,' she urged her gently, pushing her chair a little nearer the bed.

'I don't remember falling, nothing of that at all.' Anna's eyes held Jill's in concentration. 'The last thing I can recall is talking with Delia in her office, and hearing her say that we'd better get a taxi to the station, and I *think* I can remember leaving the office, but after that nothing at all, except a feeling that I was in bed—in other words, in here.'

'So you've lost about an hour in all, which isn't too bad,' Jill murmured, half to herself, then sat up straight as she heard Anna say that Mr Greerson had been up to see her during breakfast-time. 'And he said he'd been up see me before, when I was *non compos*.'

'Yes, that's true, he had.'

'He's so thoughtful, darling, especially where you're concerned. He wanted to ring you and tell you how I was, but Sister beat him to it. He was in a rush, but he stayed a few minutes, said he wouldn't be here much today. He's operating somewhere else—carving, he called it—somewhere over the river, I think he said, St Mildred's.'

'That's right, he goes there sometimes,' Jill replied, digesting this item of news.

'I asked him if he knew what had happened to Barney, and he said he was with Clive, but that his mother would have him if necessary. I thought that was very kind.'

'You're Mrs Greerson's favourite writer.'

'You mean, she's sucking up.'

'She may be.'

'That's unkind of you, Jill.'

'Yes, perhaps it is. Anyway, Barney's all right with Clive,' Jill averred doggedly. She returned to the subject of Anna's amnesia, explaining to her that, as it was only of an hour's duration, she would probably remember everything in about a month or, at most, five weeks. 'And during that time,' she added, 'you won't be advised to write; you'll have to take it easy at home, *and* you're likely to be in here for another week at least.'

'I think you're trying to cheer me up!' Anna pulled a face.

'Well, just in case this helps,' Jill went on, 'I'm going to ask if I can take my annual leave once you're discharged. We can spend it together at home, and I can keep my eye on you.'

'It'll be a busman's holiday for you,' Anna protested, but her face brightened, and Jill saw it.

'Tiresome for me, isn't it?' she said wryly, gripping her grandmother's hand.

Soon after this Jill left for Ecclestone Ward, and for the first time—when Sister Beck enquired how her grandmother was—she was able to smile and *tell* her, instead of wishing she hadn't asked.

There was a teaching round on Friday, and, as Sister was off duty, it was Jill who escorted Sir Rodney, Adam, Dick Lane and three young medics to half a dozen different beds in the ward. Dick gave a short case-history on each patient, after which Sir Rodney asked the medics questions, frightening them half to death, taking the view that what he'd had to suffer in his youth ought, in all fairness, to be their lot too. And so it was that he positively rounded on one bespectacled youth, who was staring, fascinated, at Jill's shapely legs. 'Why is there a delayed clotting time in obstructive jaundice, Renton?'

The youth jumped visibly, and Adam moved closer to Jill. 'I admire his choice of scenery,' he whispered in her ear, 'but not during a teaching round. God help him if he fluffs!'

He didn't. With the first shock over, Renton was speaking out. 'Because of lack of bile reaching the intestine, sir. Vitamin K, the clotting vitamin, can't be absorbed in the absence of bile.'

'Correct.' Sir Rodney looked disappointed, Adam amused, while Jill, whose cheeks were carnation-pink, moved quickly behind the truck of notes and wheeled it to the next bed.

By the time the round was finished the ward lunches had come down. Nurse Catling served them, helped by Nurse Bell, while Jill joined Chrissie for sausage and mash and baked beans in the nurses' dining-room. 'This is the night you're going home, isn't it?' Chrissie said, buttering a roll.

'At half-four, yes, I am, but only for one night, just to collect Anna's things really, and as I'm on lates tomorrow I shan't need to get up at the crack of dawn.'

'Do you mind staying in the house on your own?' Chrissie looked at her curiously.

'Good lord, no,' Jill said, 'Anna does it all the time. It's not at the back of beyond; there are other houses in the road. Anyway, I've been there alone plenty of times before.'

'Oh, well, that's all right, then.' Chrissie got up to fetch their coffee, ignoring Jill's protests that she wouldn't have time to enjoy it. There was so much she'd got to get through before four o'clock.

Even so, she made it, and just before half-past four was crossing the yard in her overcoat and beret, over-night bag in hand, when Adam, who had spotted her getting out of the lift, ran to catch her up. She was nearly to the gates when he managed it. 'If you're on your way home,' he said, 'I can give you a lift—the car's over there.' Without waiting for her answer, he reached for her bag, grasped her elbow, and steered her across the yard.

'This is very good of you.' She gasped a little, for the wind had an icy edge. It flicked at his tie, and blew her fringe back, setting her beret askew. As she put up a hand to straighten it she saw with a jerk of dismay that Vanessa Lawley was sitting in the rear of Adam's red

Lotus, surrounded by crate-like boxes. She rolled down the window and laughed.

'I'm not trusting your boot, Adam. This stuff's valuable!' She didn't seem at all surprised to see Jill, just asked how her grandmother was. 'It must have been a worrying time for you,' she said.

'Yes, it was at first.' Still feeling jolted at finding her there, Jill got herself into the front seat as Adam held the door. Watching him walk round the car, the brilliance of the sun showing up the red streaks in his hair, she cursed him silently. Damn it all, he might have told her he'd already got a passenger!

'Vanessa's going to work in America for two years, so she's clearing out the flat,' he remarked smoothly as the big car was sliding through the hospital gates.

'Oh, are you, Miss Lawley?' Jill found her voice, and tried to turn in her seat. Clearing out the flat. . .Was she hearing aright? What did it all mean?

'The name's Vanessa, and yes, I am. Rothenby's are sending me to the New York branch, and I couldn't be more thrilled. They've laid on an apartment for me, and everything. I fly out on Sunday.'

'*This* Sunday. . .so quickly? Fervently Jill hoped that she was making all the right noises, for she was still in a state of shock. Going for two years. . .that was ages! Did Adam mind? She dared not look at him, yet longed to do so. *Did* Adam mind?

'More like lightning than merely quickly. I only got ten days' warning. Still, that's the way it goes sometimes.' Vanessa steadied one of her cartons as it gave an ominous chink. 'I've been living at home with my parents ever since last Friday. They wanted to see a bit more of me before I actually went. I've had to commute to town, which hasn't been easy with the roads as they are. Still, I'm all ready to go now. I got rid of the car yesterday, and Adam has agreed to rent my flat till a buyer can be found.'

'It suits me to do so. I like my own place,' Adam put in at this point.

'But won't you,' Jill asked Vanessa, 'want it when you come back?'

'Oh, I doubt it. No, I'd rather sell. I can always buy something else when I come back, if I want to, that is.' Vanessa smiled a little smile that had something of smugness about it. She was certainly pleased with herself. 'I never liked it all that much, anyway. I've only owned it for eighteen months.'

'Oh, I see.' Jill faced front again. Her neck was getting a crick, but that was nothing to the tide of thoughts washing about in her head. Adam had been living in the flat on his own. . .he hadn't moved in with Vanessa. . .she had moved out. Dick Lane had been wrong, but then, he often was.

'Don't you find nursing depressing?' Vanessa asked after a pause, trying to ease herself more comfortably within her blockage of crates.

'It can be depressing,' Jill forced herself to make the right reply, 'but it can also be very reward- ing. . .satisfying too.'

'Tell me more,' Vanessa urged, and, surprised at her request, but only too willing to fill the silence, Jill gave her a little insight into life on the wards, with all its ups and downs. Taken as a whole, the journey home, which she had viewed with such dismay when she'd seen Vanessa sitting there, proved to be not too bad.

Half an hour later, once Adam had brought the Lotus to a stop in the circular drive at Homewood, he told Jill he would see her inside. 'Give me your key, and I'll just make sure everything is all right.'

She did as he asked, without thinking twice. 'Can I come too?' Vanessa asked, easing backwards out of the car. 'I've got shocking pins and needles, cramped up like this!'

They all three went into the house, which struck very cold. 'I expect Mrs Legge has been along and turned off the heating,' Jill said. She led them into the sitting-room, switched on the electric fire and offered them sherry, which Vanessa accepted but Adam refused, going, instead, on a look-about tour of the downstairs rooms.

'All men love playing Cops and Robbers,' Vanessa remarked, carrying her drink to the other side of the sitting-room, where she took a long hard look at an oil painting, a seascape, by an artist called Conan Dryden. 'Now that,' she said, 'would fetch thirty thousand, maybe more, at auction today. Conan Dryden's work is in great demand just at the moment. He was one of the early Victorian painters—but I expect Mrs Stevens knows that.'

'I'm sure she does. Anna's no fool.' Jill was a little irked by the way Vanessa's eyes were riveted on other pictures as well. Still, her speciality was paintings, Adam had mentioned that, so it was natural for her to be drawn to them. I'm just being churlish, she thought. Even so, she was angered afresh when Vanessa halted in front of a pair of water-colours and called them pretty daubs.

'They're worthless, but attractive,' she added, seeing the look on Jill's face, 'but, there again, I'm sure your grandmother is well aware of that.'

'They're mine, as a matter of fact, and they've always hung there—my father painted them. They're priceless to me,' Jill said sharply, facing Vanessa, but also seeing Adam come into the room.

'There *are* other values, Nessa, apart from intrinsic ones.' He came to stand at Jill's side, and Vanessa agreed with him very quickly as though determined not to cross swords with him

'Perhaps your father was an illustrator of some kind, perhaps for publishers?' She finished her drink very quickly and set her glass down on the tray.

'Dad was a lawyer; painting was his hobby.' Jill's eyes went back to the paintings.

'My work is my hobby, which probably,' Vanessa gave a light laugh, 'makes me a very dull girl, although even I intend to let my hair down with a vengeance tonight! My parents are giving a party for me at home, in Mountford Drive—a "farewell to our daughter" party— there'll be over fifty guests.' Of which Adam will be one, thought Jill, longing to look at him, but not daring to do so, and feeling relieved when he said they ought to go.

'I hope everything goes well for you in America, Vanessa,' she managed to say at the door.

'Oh, it will, thanks.' Vanessa's reply was tossed off, light as air. 'I'm tailor-made for the post, which perhaps sounds conceited, but, you see, I know my worth.'

Just as you know the worth of everything else, including Anna's pictures, Jill thought, watching her go down the steps and stand by the Lotus, waiting for Adam to unlock its doors. He did so, waving a hand to Jill over its roof. 'Go inside and get warm.' His words came back to her, blown on the wind, and she waved back, but stood at the open front door till she could no longer see the big red car moving along the hedge.

Back in the sitting-room, she sat for some time huddled in front of the fire. Vanessa was going to be away for two years, so did that signify the end of things between her and Adam, or would he write to her, and see her when she came home on visits, which she was almost certain to do? He's been so wonderful to me. . .ever since Monday, she thought. Was that solely because he was sorry about Anna and wanted to comfort me? Or—and this was a beastly, unworthy, serpent-like thought—was he hoping. . .*is* he hoping that, once

Vanessa has gone, I'll fill the gap, take on where she left off?

The arrival of Clive, who had promised to bring Barney over for the evening, effectively stopped her thinking of Adam, at least for a little while. The little dog was overjoyed to see her, jumping up into her arms, then scouring the house for his mistress, returning, a little downcast, to Clive, who lifted him and set him on his knee. 'Actually, he's settled down fine,' he said, 'but I think if I take his bed back with me he'll feel even more at home. When will Mrs Stevens be out of hospital?'

'I would think in about a week or ten days,' replied Jill. 'She'll want Barney back with her then, of course, and I hope to take some of my holiday, till she's able to cope on her own.'

They continued to talk of Anna for a while, after which Jill made a scratch supper—bacon and eggs, followed by fruit and cheese—while Clive got the gas-boiler alight, and the house began to get warm.

After their meal he went off, carrying Barney and his bed to the car. 'If you're going back to the hospital tomorrow morning you'll have things to do,' he said.

Jill agreed that this was so. 'But thanks for your help.' She switched on the hall light. 'Almost the first thing Anna asked me was who had Barney. She was glad it was you. *I'm* grateful too; it's such a load off my mind.'

'Well, I owed you, didn't I?' He grinned. 'And, even if I hadn't, I'd still have obliged—I'm a nice chap! Bye, then, for now.'

Off he went, but soon after that Miss Perry from over the way—an inveterate chatterer—called to ask how Anna was. 'I heard the news from Mrs Legge! My *dear*, how terrible!' She stayed for over an hour, talking incessantly all the while. By the time she had gone and Jill had packed a case for Anna it was after ten and,

feeling bone tired, she did the rounds of the house—
locking up, setting the burglar alarm, switching off
electric plugs. Living in a house, she reflected, was a far
cry indeed from living in a flat in the nurses' home,
where responsibility was nil. It was a great deal more
quiet, too. There were no human sounds. She didn't
exactly *mind* the silence, but felt it so acutely that it was
almost a noise in itself, and not peaceful at all.

It was some time before she went to sleep, and when
she eventually did so, it was to dream that the hospital
was on fire, and that Adam was trapped in the operating
theatre, and no one would cross the sterile boundary to
try to get him out. A bell like a fire bell was
ringing continuously, a clamorous metallic sound—
kararr. . .kararr. . .kararr. . .kararr. The din was in
Jill's head as she struggled and strained to get to Adam,
as she tried to move her feet, which refused to lift, which
were heavy and weighted, and the noise of the bell went
on.

It became louder; surely it was louder, she was
surfacing, waking up. Kararr. . .kararr. . .kararr. . .
kararr. Then realisation struck, sharp, like an arrow,
piercing her awake. It was here, in the house—it was the
burglar alarm! Someone had broken in! The lights that
operated with the alarm were flashing out into the night.
It was true, it was true! It was really happening! Jill
flung herself out of bed. She locked her door as she told
herself, Never go downstairs, never tackle a burglar
yourself! She dragged on her dressing-gown, found her
mules, felt the back of her neck go stiff. But the police
would be coming—she knew they would, for when the
alarm went off an alert went through to them as well.
They would come; they could soon be here.

She went to the window and pulled back the curtains.
Lights were springing up in several of the houses
opposite; she wasn't really alone. Yet she was fright-

ened. . .dear God, she was frightened, so frightened that her heart beat louder than the sound of the bell, for supposing he came upstairs? Supposing he was mad, and broke down the door. . .supposing he had a knife? She thought of rape, and was just about to move furniture across the door, when she saw the car with 'Police' on its top tearing into the drive.

She flew down the stairs, feet scarcely touching them, and unbolted the door. In came a policewoman, followed by two constables, one of them holding a black Alsatian on a short, thick lead. If they hadn't immediately stepped inside Jill would have dragged them in. She had never been so frantically relieved to have uniformed company.

'Are you all right, Mrs Stevens?' The policewoman took her arm and sat her down, while Jill explained that she wasn't Mrs Stevens, also who she was and why she was there, and turned off the alarm.

One of the officers raced round the back, taking the dog and the other searched the house; then they searched it together, eventually joining their female colleague in the kitchen, where she had made Jill some tea. 'There's no sign of a break-in, Miss Arbor, and nothing has been disturbed in an obvious way, so far as we can see, but perhaps before we go you'd like to have a look round,' the older policeman said.

Jill did so with Sheila, the WPC, at her side. 'I'm sure you're right,' she said as they came back downstairs. 'No one's been in. I'd know if they had; there'd be a different kind of feeling, and everything's in its place. I've wasted your time, haven't I, but *why did the alarm go off*?'

'They're fairly easily triggered, miss. We've known it happen before.' The younger policeman smiled at her and resettled his cap. 'What we'll do is ring the company for you, get them to check it up.'

'It's Safehomes Ltd,' Jill supplied. 'My grandmother had it installed about three weeks or a month ago.'

'Ah, it's new?'

'Fairly new, yes.'

'Well, we'll get them to call tomorrow—or today, I suppose I should say.' It was the dog handler speaking this time, and it was exactly twelve-fifteen, Jill saw, glancing quickly towards the grandfather clock.

'I shall be leaving for London just before eleven tomorrow,' she said. 'I nurse there, and my grandmother won't be back for another week.'

Making a note of all this and promising that a rep from Safehomes would call early on, they all trooped to the front door, the black dog making a prick-eared shadow on the wall. 'If you're nervous, Miss Arbor,' the policewoman said, turning back to her, 'I can stay here with you, you know. You don't have to be alone.'

'I've wasted too much of your time as it is, and I'll be just fine,' Jill managed to say, shuddering a little as cold air rushed into the hall. It was then that she spotted two neighbours coming up the drive, while down the road, slamming out of a car that she instantly recognised, was Adam. . .*Adam*! It was all she could do not to rush out and into his arms, except that her legs were heavy and weighted, like those in her dream, and simply wouldn't move.

'What's happened? What's going on?' She never really knew if Adam shouted that, or if one of the neighbours did, or if they'd all said it in chorus, their shocked faced upturned to the door.

The police went off, stripping the scene of much of its drama. The neighbours were asked in, and reassured, after which they, too, took their leave, murmuring among themselves. Only Adam stayed, closing the door. Jill saw him coming towards her, saw his mouth moving. He was saying something, but she couldn't hear what it was. All sound was going, and his face was dwindling. . .dwindling and dwindling. . .then the black mists closed in, the floor tilted and turned, and she pitched forward into obliterating dark.

When she came to she was in the sitting-room, lying on the couch. Adam was sitting on the edge of it, chafing her hands and wrists. 'That's more like it,' he said as she opened her eyes, seeing, first, the familiar room swinging into focus, then only him, only his face, which was nearly as ashen as hers.

She made to sit up and he helped her, an arm about her waist.

'How do you feel?' He moved a little away from her on the couch.

'OK, all right, but how stupid of me—I've never passed out before.'

'Stay where you are for a minute or two—I'll fetch you some water.' He found his way, blundering a little, along to the kitchen. Returning to the sitting-room with a cup of water. . .he couldn't find any glasses. . .he watched her sip it, saw her shaking hands, heard the rim of the cup hit her teeth. 'Now, look,' he said, 'I'm staying here, I'm not leaving you like this. And there's no need to worry. . .' he smiled a little when he saw her startled face '. . .I shan't try anything on—I do have *some* morals! I'm staying to look after you. . .you've nothing to fear from me.'

'I don't fear you,' she said, but she didn't think he'd heard her, for he'd gone to fetch the car off the road. He was gone some minutes, and when he returned he said he'd sleep downstairs.

'Like that I can be night watchman, and woe to all burglars!' He was determined to jest, which annoyed her.

'There aren't any burglars,' she said, 'and if you're staying then it'll be in the guest room—couches are murder to sleep on.' One of her mules had slipped off, and he bent down and put it back on, holding her small neat foot in his hand, smiling up at her.

'There you are, Cinderella, *and* it's way past midnight. Now, are you going to be able to walk, or do you want carrying?'

Anyone would think I was a troublesome parcel, she thought as she told him that she didn't think she'd be bothering him by fainting again tonight. So the stairs were ascended sedately and separately, he walking behind.

'This is the guest-room.' She crossed the wide landing. 'You'll find everything in it you need, and there's an *en suite* bathroom, which is very convenient.'

'I didn't expect five-star treatment,' he said as she flicked on the light, and his eyes took in the grey-carpeted room with its primrose curtains and puffy yellow duvets on the two single beds. 'In fact, I'm beginning to wonder who is looking after whom.'

'Anna would expect me to look after a guest.' She handed him two towels from the airing cupboard. 'Good-night, then, Adam, and thank you for staying here.'

'I'm glad I was passing.' They nodded at one another, he calling out, 'Sleep well,' as she went towards her door.

But she didn't sleep well; she didn't sleep at all; and unknown to her, in the room across the landing. . .neither did he.

CHAPTER TWELVE

JILL was downstairs soon after seven, pulling the curtains back and looking out on to a morning of streaming rain and wind—a mad March day, if ever there was one. She was glad the heating was on. Her face bore little trace of her sleepless night; her bright hair cheered up the morning, and her eyes were clear and unshadowed. Spruce in her uniform, she moved about the kitchen, making coffee and cutting bread.

Adam was still in the guest bathroom. She had heard the hum of the shaver as she had crossed the landing; he would probably want to get home as soon as he could. She knew he was off duty for the whole weekend, whereas she was on at midday, and must make tracks for town as soon as the man from Safehomes had been. She hoped he wouldn't be late.

She wouldn't make the toast until Adam came down. She wondered how he had slept. I certainly hope better than I did, she thought. I couldn't stop thinking about him, and I can't now, which is quite ridiculous. He had cared enough to stay with her last night, but had made it very clear that he was simply looking after her, and that nothing else was on board. He needn't have spelled it out quite so plainly—it wasn't necessary. What puzzled her was how he'd been passing her gate at that time of night. He'd been going to Vanessa's party at Bexford, which was three miles off. Still, perhaps after the party he'd helped ferry some guests home. Vanessa had implied that half the county would be going, and the county included Windon. That must have been how it was, Jill thought, jumping to her feet as she heard the unmistakable sound of him coming downstairs. She went into the hall to meet him.

'I hope you slept well.' She smiled, her heart leaping at the sight of him, immaculate in his dark suit, hair damp from the shower, blue eyes smiling at her.

'What's more important, how are you?' he asked, following her into the kitchen, where the coffee percolator was jerking out fragrant billows of steam.

'Oh, I'm fine,' she said, 'never been better, and I slept like a log. Now, if you'd rather have tea than coffee, say so.' Lying was making her brusque.

'Coffee's my favourite.'

'And there are eggs, if you'd like some scrambled with your toast. You must make a good breakfast before you go home. I owe you that, at least.' She could hear herself being less than gracious. Oh, if only she didn't feel so tight and twitchy—it was like being threaded with wires.

'Toast is all I ever have, thanks.' Adam watched honey and jam, marmalade and a dish of butter being set on the table at speed. 'But I hadn't planned to go home, actually. I thought we'd drive up to town together.' Jill had her back to him now, arranging wholemeal bread under the grill. 'You see,' he went on, 'I've got to get my furniture into the flat. Up to the moment I've virtually been camping in the place.'

'Isn't Vanessa's furniture there?' She tried not to sound too surprised.

'No, no, it's an unfurnished let. . .that's what I prefer. What time is your security man coming?' He was changing the subject, she thought.

'Soon after eight-thirty, I hope,' she loaded toast into the rack, 'and I'm on duty at twelve midday, so it's going to be a rush.'

'I'll get you there, don't worry.' Adam rose, and seated her at the table, passing her the butter as though she, not he, were the guest. He had lovely manners, perfect manners, and he knew how to treat a woman. Jill poured the coffee, praying that she wouldn't shoot it all over the cloth.

As they ate their breakfast in the warm, pleasant kitchen, the wind-driven rain flinging against the window, he encouraged her to tell him a little more about her fright of the night before. 'Were you asleep when the alarm went off?'

'Yes, I was,' she said, 'and somehow that made it so much worse. I couldn't, for a second, think what it was, and then, when I did, I was numb with terror, then galvanised by it—locking my door, rushing to the window, pulling back the curtains, wishing I could jump out. Still. . .' she smiled at him, making a little movement with her hands '. . .I needn't have worried; the police came quickly, no one had broken in, and the neighbours came, and you came.' She smiled at him again, unreservedly this time, for she was feeling less nervous of him. 'I've never really thanked you properly, have I, for putting yourself out, and for staying with me? So I'm doing it now. Thank you; I shan't forget.'

'Jill, my *dear*. . .' He half-rose, then sank back as the telephone rang. Jill went to answer it, coming back to said that Safehomes were calling at nine.

'And Adam, I've been thinking, as we're going straight up to town, wouldn't you like to ring Mrs Greerson? I mean, won't she be worrying. . .wondering where you've been all night?'

He laughed then, *really* laughed, tipping back his head. 'Oh, I'm a big boy now,' he said, 'but I've done what I should. I rang her last night from the phone in my car when I fetched it off the road.'

'Oh, well, that's all right, then.' Still reacting from his laugh, she said a little pointedly, 'I expect you woke her up.'

'I didn't, as it happened—she'd only just got in from the Lawleys' party.'

'But I thought. . .Wasn't that where *you*'d been?' Jill swallowed a corner of toast with watering eyes as she struggled not to choke.

'No, no, I'd been to the Farnes'—to dinner with Charles and his wife. That's how I came to be passing by at that late hour. They live in Merricks Close, just off from here. Well, you know that, of course. Strikes me it's a bit too far from the Walbrook, but Charles doesn't seem to mind.'

Jill's thoughts whirled. 'I know Mrs Farne by sight,' she managed to say. Adam nodded, but seemed to be choosing his words with infinite care.

'As I passed here on my way to their house,' he was looking intently at her, 'I couldn't help noticing that you had a visitor. I saw a car in the drive.'

'Clive's car.'

'I thought it was.'

'He came for Barney's bed, and got the central heating going. He's a very good friend to have.'

'I think he's still carrying a torch for you.'

'Absolutely not! I'd know if he were!' She collected the plates and took them to the sink. Adam said nothing, and for some reason this made her flash round and say, 'Perhaps *you're* carrying one for Vanessa and can't bear to see her go!'

'You've been listening to gossip.' He rose from his chair and stood in front of her.

'Most people do.'

'That's very true.' He was cupping her shoulder, gently smoothing the thick white cotton of her dress. 'But one and one,' he went on slowly, 'don't always make a pair. I met Nessa through my mother's being on friendly terms with the Lawleys. I found her easy to talk to, amusing. I admired her striking looks, but they didn't excite me; I wasn't drawn to her; there was no sexual pull, no what your grandmother would describe as a vital spark. When we met it was usually at her home or mine, and when I got my post at the Walbrook we met for a drink occasionally. That's how I came to be offered her flat, which will do me very well for a time. So you see, darling, any gossip you heard wasn't founded on fact. I'm not saying,' he looked at her closely, 'that there haven't been women. . .occasionally. . .along the way, but not all that many, and not Vanessa, and not anyone for a long time.'

'This seems to be a morning for revelations.' Suddenly shy of him, Jill couldn't meet his eyes, and he didn't make her, just laid his cheek on her hair.

'There are more.' His voice was hoarse, and urgent, warm against her ear. 'I love you, Jill, and I think you know it. I simply cannot believe that I haven't shown it, time and again. I love and want you so!'

'I love you too. . .oh, I love you too!' Her arms moved round his back, and she held him fast, held him close, hugged him to herself. When she moved her face his mouth was on hers so quickly that she gasped, then the world rocked as she kissed him back, while somewhere, a long way off, her dream of marriage, of being with the same man forever and ever, rolled away, as dreams often did when they hit the light of day. One day Adam would leave her, he didn't want the marriage commitment. They would be dear lovers, but one day she would lose him. She moved, and he loosed her at once.

'What's wrong?' he asked.

'Not a thing, just a goose walking over my grave once again.'

'Then marry me, and we'll keep every goose firmly in his place.'

'But Adam, you don't want to be married, you told me that ages ago!' She leaned back in his arms, looking shocked, looking incredulous.

'A man can be wrong. I do want it with you, more than I can say. I've been in love with you since Boxing night, when we walked home under the lamps, but it wasn't until after Seftonbridge, it wasn't until last week, when we tried to maintain a chilly front and be simply doctor and nurse, that I realised the extent of my feeling for you, had a taste of how I'd feel if I lost you, if you walked right out of my life. I knew then that I must gather my courage and find out if you felt the same, so on the day Sister Beck came back—you know, when you dropped the cake—I made up my mind to invite you out to dinner and ask you to marry me. But then Mrs Stevens had her accident and you were out of your mind with worry, so I couldn't do it, I had to bide my time. Well, now I've bided it.' He smiled, but looked anxious. 'So will you please marry me, and make me the happiest man in the world?'

Jill touched his face; it was hard to speak, then the words overflowed. 'Oh, I will, Adam. . .I will, I will!' She went into his arms. And this time when he held her, as well as the joy of it all, as well as the tide of passion that swept them along like a sea, she had a feeling of safety, of having come home. She had found the man of her dreams.

The man from Safehomes came and went, telling them that he thought the alarm had been triggered by the central heating, but that he would stop this happening again by a small alteration which his firm would make once Anna was home. He was fairly blasé about it, but so, also, was Jill. It was strange how little things like burglar alarms going off and scaring her stiff ceased to matter now that she and Adam were engaged.

They were married at Easter, three weeks later, in

Windon Register Office. They had wanted a quiet wedding, but crowds of their friends turned up.

Anna, whose memory was fully restored, was delighted about the match. Elaine Greerson, who had nursed a faint hope that Adam would marry Vanessa, was a little less over the moon, but consoled herself with the thought that Jill was a decent girl with a famous grandmother, which counted for a great deal.

Jill kept on nursing for a little while, but once the Barbican flat was sold, and she and Adam moved into their own house on Highgate Hill, she worked part-time only until she became pregnant with their first child, who, to the great delight of both of them, turned out to be twins.

— MEDICAL ❤ ROMANCE —

The books for enjoyment this month are:

SAVING DR GREGORY Caroline Anderson
FOR LOVE'S SAKE ONLY Margaret Barker
THE WRONG DIAGNOSIS Drusilla Douglas
ENCOUNTER WITH A SURGEON Janet Ferguson

❤　❤　❤　❤　❤

Treats in store!

Watch next month for the following absorbing
stories:

THE SINGAPORE AFFAIR Kathleen Farrell
CAROLINE'S CONQUEST Hazel Fisher
A PLACE OF REFUGE Margaret Holt
THAT SPECIAL JOY Betty Beaty

Available from Boots, Martins, John Menzies, W.H. Smith,
most supermarkets and other paperback stockists.

Also available from Mills & Boon Reader Service,
P.O. Box 236, Thornton Road, Croydon, Surrey CR9 3RU.

Readers in South Africa - write to:
Book Services International Ltd, P.O. Box 41654,
Craighall, Transvaal 2024.

Mills & Boon

Discover the thrill of 4 Exciting Medical Romances – FREE

FREE BOOKS FOR YOU

In the exciting world of modern
medicine, the emotions of true love
have an added drama. Now you can
experience four of these
unforgettable romantic tales of passion
and heartbreak FREE – and look forward to
a regular supply of Mills & Boon
Medical Romances delivered direct to your door!

☙ ☙ ☙

Turn the page for details of 2 extra
free gifts, and how to apply.

An Irresistible Offer from Mills & Boon

Here's an offer from Mills & Boon to become a regular reader of Medical Romances. To welcome you, we'd like you to have four books, a cuddly teddy and a special MYSTERY GIFT, all absolutely free and without obligation.

Then, every month you could look forward to receiving 4 more **brand new** Medical Romances for £1.60 each, delivered direct to your door, post and packing free. Plus our newsletter featuring author news, competitions, special offers, and lots more. This invitation comes with no strings attached. You can cancel or suspend your subscription at any time, and still keep your free books and gifts.

Its so easy. Send no money now. Simply fill in the coupon below and post it at once to -

**Mills & Boon Reader Service, FREEPOST,
PO Box 236, Croydon, Surrey CR9 9EL**

NO STAMP REQUIRED

- -

YES! Please rush me my 4 Free Medical Romances and 2 Free Gifts! Please also reserve me a Reader Service Subscription. If I decide to subscribe, I can look forward to receiving 4 brand new Medical Romances every month for just £6.40, delivered direct to my door. Post and packing is free, and there's a free Mills & Boon Newsletter. If I choose not to subscribe I shall write to you within 10 days - I can keep the books and gifts whatever I decide. I can cancel or suspend my subscription at any time. I am over 18.

EP20D

Name (Mr/Mrs/Ms) _____

Address _____

_____

_____ Postcode _____

Signature _____